A COUNCIL OF ANGELS

BOOK ONE OF THE COUNCIL OF ANGELS SERIES

SEAN MARSHALL

TO THE
READS OF
COMMON SENSE!

Sam Harris

ALSO BY SEAN MARSHALL

Council of Angels Series

～

A Friend of Angels - Prequel Novella
A Family of Angels - Book Two
A Legacy of Angels - Book Three

Go to SeanMarshall.com for more details

A Council of Angels

Copyright © 2019 by Sean Marshall

All Rights Reserved. No portion of this book may be reproduced in any form without permission from the publisher, except as permitted by U.S. copyright law.

This is a work of fiction. Names, characters, businesses, places, events, and incidents are either the products of the author's imagination or are used in a fictitious manner. Any resemblance to actual persons, living or dead, or actual events, businesses, or locales is purely coincidental.

This book does not directly reflect the author's personal, religious, or philosophical views.

ISBN: 978-1-955530-08-8 (ebook) | ISBN: 978-1-955530-09-5 (paperback)

Cover Design: 100covers.com

Photo Credits: Baranov E/Shutterstock.com

Published by Lark Lane Media

To order, or for more information, visit SeanMarshall.com

∼

To Heidi—thank you for your incredible patience & tremendous faith. I owe you at least 17 ½ foot rubs.

PART I

TO BELIEVE

CHAPTER ONE

Have you ever seen an angel? I have. But for me it's cheating because, well, I am one. I wasn't always an angel, though. It's a pretty interesting story. I never thought something like this would happen to me.

But wait, I'm getting distracted. This isn't my story. This is a story about a young man named Bass. Well, his real name is actually Sebastian Joseph Martinez. I think you'll agree it's a fine name.

What you have in your hands is a collection of my notes. A report, actually. I was asked to put this together for you, my sweetest friend, and this is my best attempt at creating a narrative based on the events I personally witnessed.

In my first assigned case as a guardian angel, I got the role of what the others called "secretary angel." I'm very proud of this. In trying hard to be a good secretary angel, I did my best to record everything I thought was important to the case.

I should let you know, in a way I can't fully explain, I was able to be present for everything I'm about to share with you. It was part of my duties as a secretary angel. At some points I could interact with Bass directly, but most of the time, I simply observed. Some people say it's like being a "fly on the wall." In my case, it was more like "an invisible angel standing on the side of a room...or sitting in a car...or floating in the ocean..." or something like that.

I also had access to the thoughts of others, especially Bass's. Now, as I try to piece together this report for you, I'll include some of those thoughts, as they relate specifically to this case. But I'll also try to write this as officially as I can, keeping my own commentary to a minimum.

Throughout this report, I'll include a few of my own memos I sent to the team while on the assignment because I feel they add some insight to the work we did with Bass.

As you'll soon find out, this case was very special for me. I'm providing you with this background on Bass to help you better understand your own present circumstances. Perhaps learning more about him can help you better understand your own journey. That's my hope at least.

I humbly ask for your patience. I'm just an angel. In no way do I claim to be an author.

CHAPTER TWO

I want to tell you about Bass, but I think I should first tell you about a man named Dan. It's not a happy way to start out, but it's where the story really begins. Here we go.

Dan Johnson, an electrician living in Fountain Valley, California, turned 63 years old at the very moment he lost his job. It was the first day of April at 4:34 p.m., the exact time of his birth, when his boss gave him the news. He was with the company for over 25 years and they chose this day, of all days, to let him go.

"We're really sorry," said Dan's boss, and owner of the company. "We have to make some big cutbacks and today was the day we needed to let everyone know." The boss paused and said, "I'm not sure if this helps, but you're not the only one."

Dan couldn't believe his ears. He sat in a chair in front of his boss's desk, staring down at his steel toe boots. His eyes followed the work-worn creases in the leather as all of his hard work flashed through his mind—the years of grueling labor, the thousands of jobs he'd done, the younger electricians shirking their assignments, everything. Now it was ending.

"We do have a severance package for you," the boss said as he slid an envelope across the desk. "It's not as much as we were hoping to give you, especially because of all of your time with the company, but it's the best we can do right now."

Dan slowly reached for the envelope that contained his last check. It seemed so thin as he held it in his rough, gnarled fingers.

"John will go outside with you to collect all of your gear and to see you out."

With nothing left to say, Dan shook hands with his boss and walked out of the office. Feeling like he was headed to the electric chair, he shuffled with slumped shoulders and bit his lip to keep it from quivering. He looked to the front door of the company building where John, the boss's nephew, stood with his arms behind his back as if awaiting the order to flip the switch.

As Dan passed the front desk, he stopped to look at Cindy, the front office manager who was already wiping tears from her eyes with a crumpled up tissue. She stood up and crashed into Dan, hugging him tightly.

"I'm so sorry!" she said.

Dan struggled to find his voice. "It's…it's OK," he stammered.

"I got this for you," Cindy sniffed. "We were going to have a party for you after everyone got back in. I didn't know this was going to happen."

Cindy handed him a card that had a few employee signatures on it.

"I'm sorry I didn't get everyone to sign it." Cindy grabbed another tissue and carefully wiped the mascara from her eyes.

Dan stared at the card. Everything he'd worked for was suddenly summed up in a half-signed, generic birthday card.

"We have a cake for you in the fridge. I picked it up last night. It's an ice cream cake."

"It's OK. I need to go," he said, and gave her a quick hug.

"Thank you for always helping me so much." Dan said. "I couldn't have found all of those job sites without you."

It wasn't as impactful as Dan hoped, but it was the best he had at the moment. He turned to the front door, where John still stood as serious as ever.

With a quick transfer of tools, equipment, and keys, Dan relinquished everything that represented his livelihood for over two decades. John extended his hand. "Best of luck."

Dan shook hands with John and turned around to get into his truck. As he started the engine, his phone beeped with a message from his wife, Nancy. "Can you please pick up bread & dog food on the way home?"

Dan sent a quick text back. "Yeah, no problem."

He pulled onto the road towards the store and everything started to sink in. What was he going to do now? What would he say to Nancy? They were already struggling. And their marriage reflected it. With a meager sum in the way of retirement, it was a daily conversation between them.

A few minutes later, Dan turned into the parking lot. He thought about trying to get another job quickly. Where would he start? Could he get another job? Who would hire him? Was he too old?

He steered the truck into a parking space and turned it off. He looked into the rearview mirror, examining his face. The lines on his eyes were prominent and the afternoon sun highlighted every single gray hair.

He took a deep breath and went into the store. After grabbing the bread and dog food, he found himself in front of the beer cooler and, without thinking, picked up a 12-pack. He wasn't a big drinker, but he occasionally had a beer with friends at parties or BBQs, but rarely bought alcohol on his own.

After checking out and walking to his truck, Dan threw the bread and dog food inside. When he lifted the pack of beer, the handle began tearing. He lifted faster, but it ripped open, spilling cans onto the asphalt.

He cursed as one of the cans punctured, spewing beer over his boots. He grabbed it, getting beer on his hands, which he licked off. Without thinking, he sucked the rest of the beer out of the can and then threw it into the back of the truck.

After wiping his hands, he picked up the remaining cans of beer and stared at them on his seat.

"Why not?" he said out loud. "After all, it is my birthday."

For a moment, he held a can in his hand, thinking about what he was about to do. He looked around, glanced at himself again in the mirror, and then justified his actions. He'd just stay put and call Nancy to come get him later. She'd understand.

He cracked open a can and guzzled it down. He pulled out his phone to text Nancy but dropped it. Instead of picking it up, he reached for another beer.

The light in the sky was fading when Dan looked in the mirror again. He could hardly focus. He thought for sure that Nancy was coming for him. But then he thought he needed to get to her. He needed to tell her about losing his job. And the dog would be hungry.

He looked to the passenger's side and noticed empty cans scattered on the seat and floor. Then he remembered the dog. It was hungry. He needed to get it food. And he needed to tell Nancy about something. His job.

Dan started the truck, pulled out of the parking lot, and tried hard to stay in his lane. He knew he wasn't far from home. If he could just make it off the busy road, he'd be set. Car horns blared at him as he grabbed the steering wheel, jarring the truck back into the correct lane. He pressed on the gas pedal, speeding up faster than intended.

Suddenly, he saw a bright light in the road directly ahead of him. He quickly swung the truck the other way and then heard a loud crunch and the sound of steel on concrete. His truck slowed down, grinding against something.

In a panic, he hit the brakes hard and came to a screeching halt. His head smashed into the steering wheel. More car horns honked. Something warm dripped down his nose.

A COUNCIL OF ANGELS

Dan threw open the door, swinging his body out. His leg lost its footing, and he fell down to the asphalt below. His eyelids felt heavy.

The sound of cars driving by filled his ears. He turned his head towards the front of the truck and saw something there. He struggled to focus. His eyelids pushed down, and he struggled to keep them open.

His head was so heavy. He strained to focus his eyes. There, under his truck, he saw a man and a motorcycle. His eyelids pushed even harder.

He closed them.

CHAPTER THREE

Bass's longtime best friend, JP, stepped into the hospital hallway to send a text to Bass's mother, Kathy. He quickly typed the message.

"Tried calling but got your voicemail. You're probably at work. Bass was in an accident. He's fine. Just some wicked road rash. They say he can leave tomorrow. Please call when you get a chance."

The return text came quickly.

"Hi JP, yes hilarious. I get it. April Fool's, right?"

"I'm not kidding. Sorry. Bass really got hit. Some drunk driver in a truck. But like I said, he's OK. They're watching him for the night."

"I'm at work right now. Are you serious? You're not just being funny?"

"Yes, but really, he's OK. I thought you would want to know. He probably wouldn't even tell you."

"Yes, OK. Thank you JP. I'll call you ASAP."

Another message came immediately.

"You're a good friend, JP. Thank you."

A COUNCIL OF ANGELS

After reading the text, JP looked up to see a police officer walking towards him.

CHAPTER FOUR

"Hey, it's good to see you waking up," a voice said.

Bass opened his eyes to see a middle-aged woman in green scrubs adjusting his bed to a sitting position. She smiled when their eyes met. She had spiky orange hair with light blue eyes and red lipstick.

"The doctor will be in soon," she said.

Bass winced with pain and looked down to see bandages covering his left leg. He moved it, and a wave of needles stabbed into his skin.

"Where am I?" he asked. "I mean, what happened?"

The nurse finished pushing buttons on a monitor by Bass's head just as the doctor came in. She said, "I'll let the doc explain."

A small woman approached Bass, carrying a file in her hand. She wore scrubs with a white lab coat, which was too big for her.

"Hi Sebastian, how are you feeling?" Dr. Wu said.

"I'm fine. Just confused."

"Any pain?"

"Yeah, a little in my leg."

Dr. Wu scribbled a couple of quick notes in the register.

Meanwhile, the nurse filled up a pitcher of water at the sink. The doctor put the file down and checked Bass's pulse.

"Long story short," she began, "you were hit by a drunk driver in a truck on Beach Blvd at around 6:15 p.m. this evening. You passed out at the scene and you were brought here where we treated your leg. You also suffered a slight concussion."

"What's wrong with my leg?"

"Actually, not much. You received some abrasions on your left leg and that's about it. Nothing's broken and no muscle tissue was damaged." She could tell Bass wasn't following. "Road rash—you got some nasty road rash. We put some fancy ointment on there to help with the healing. Besides maybe some light scarring, you'll be fine."

"What about the concussion? Isn't that a bad thing?"

"We'll run a few tests to be sure, but basically, you need to rest and be off your feet for a few days." Dr. Wu looked at the monitor next to Bass and scribbled more notes. "We're going to have you stay the night for observation, but tomorrow morning you can go home. I'll be back to check on you in a little while." She touched Bass's arm, smiled, and said, "It could have been a lot worse."

Off to the side, Bass saw the nurse nodding her head in agreement.

Dr. Wu turned to leave the room just as JP entered, along with a police officer. The officer looked young, but his mustache added a few years. Perhaps that was his intent.

"Sebast—" the officer started.

"We all call him Bass," JP interrupted. "You know, like the fish."

The cop pursed his lips, nodded, but didn't mind being corrected.

"Bass, my name is Officer Curtis Gilbert, and I need a quick minute with you if that's OK."

Bass nodded his head. He tried to remember how fast he was

going. The cop seemed to read his mind and said, "Don't worry, you were going under the speed limit. You were also wearing your helmet, which may have saved your life. Take a look."

The officer lifted the helmet and showed Bass a large gash.

"Look at this line," he began. Bass could see a huge gash that ran along the side of his helmet.

"This is where a part of the undercarriage of the truck connected with your head as the truck pushed both you and your bike along the road."

"Wow," was all Bass could get out. JP lifted his eyebrows and smiled. The nurse was sorting pillow cases in the corner, trying her best to eavesdrop without looking too obvious.

"Can you remember the last thing you saw?" the officer asked.

Bass thought for a minute and did his best to describe everything. He remembered driving down Beach Blvd after picking up a few things at a grocery store. Traffic was normal. Right after going through an intersection, he saw cars swerving in front of him. The last thing he could remember was a blinding light, which he now assumed must have been the headlights of the truck.

"Do you remember what lane you were in?"

"Yes, I was in the far left lane."

"Great," the cop said and jotted a few things down in his notepad. "Do you have any questions for me?"

"Yeah, so a drunk guy hit me?" Bass felt dumb for asking, but he was still trying to process everything.

"Yes. He's an older gentleman who was well over the legal limit. He swerved through three lanes and then into oncoming traffic where he collided with you." The cop hooked his thumbs into his belt, letting his fingers dangle on his waist.

"The good thing is that you were just coming through an intersection off a red light so you weren't moving very fast. Also, there were tire marks showing that the driver swerved last minute, so he actually hit you at an angle. Your bike took the brunt of it, causing you to spin where your head was dragged underneath. It would have been worse if he'd hit you head on going full speed."

Bass glared down at the bandages on his leg and clenched his fists.

A drunk driver...who does that? he thought. *What a total lack of self-control.*

He took a deep breath and glanced over at JP who shrugged and gave him a look like, "Whaddya gonna do?"

"What happened to the drunk?" he asked.

"He was treated for a light cut above his eye and is being held at our station."

"What now?"

The officer took a card from a pouch on his belt and handed it to Bass. "It's probably not a happy future for the guy. What's the best way to contact you?"

"Email," Bass said. "I'm always online, except when I get hit by drunk drivers."

The officer didn't smile. "What's your email address?"

Bass gave it to him and noticed the cop was writing with his left hand. He always thought left-handed people were artists and actors, not cops. The officer looked up and said, "We'll be in touch." With that, he left.

JP moved in closer and laughed.

"Dude, I can't believe you got nailed by a truck! And all you have to show for it will be some crusty scabs."

"Yeah. I know. It's nuts. It doesn't seem real."

"I told your mom what happened."

"What? Why? It's not a big deal. I don't want her to worry."

"Seriously? You were just in an accident. Everyone knows it's one of the codes in the Book of Friendship to notify moms of any accidents." JP pulled out his phone and said, "Yes, here it is. Code 382.5 line 7 'if any punk is hit on the head and dragged down the street by a drunk driver, the best friend of said punk is required to call his mother immediately, etc, etc.' See? It's all there. It's official."

Bass chuckled. "OK, buddy." Then he asked, "Did she say she's coming? You know she's gonna want to come down and make sure everything's fine."

"Don't know. She said she'd call as soon as she can. I just texted her like 5 minutes ago."

"You texted I was in an accident?"

"Dude, I tried calling first, but she didn't answer. I figured she was at work. Which she was, thank you very much."

"Fine," Bass said. "I'll call her. Do I have my phone?" Bass realized for the first time he was wearing nothing but a hospital gown. He looked at the nurse. "Do you know where my stuff is?"

"Yes," she said. "Everything is in here." She opened a dresser drawer and removed the phone. "I'll leave this here for when you'd like to call your mom." She put the phone on the stand next to the bed and then put a pillow under his leg.

"Can I get you anything else right now? Maybe some water?"

"No, thank you," Bass said. "I'm fine."

The nurse leaned in closer and looked at him directly. Her eyes appeared to sparkle. In a quiet but firm voice, she said, "Someone's watching out for you. You've been given a special gift. The question is, what will you do with it?"

She smiled and left the room.

CHAPTER FIVE

Bass opened his eyes but quickly closed them, desperately trying to cling to his dream. He was in high school again watching JP play football on a Friday night. He sat in the bleachers together with his parents, Kathy and Joe. Next to him, a girl sat with her arm through his. Bass couldn't make out her face, but it didn't matter. They had a strong connection, and her positivity made him feel whole.

He looked over at his mom, who smiled back. His dad looked at the girl and then gave Bass an approving nod. With everyone together, Bass breathed in deeply, filling his chest as he savored the moment.

Suddenly, a pain scorched into his left leg like someone cutting into it with a knife. He opened his eyes, crying out in pain, and looked down to see blood seeping through the white bandages on his leg and onto the sheets.

He laid his head back on his pillow while the pain subsided. He thought of his dream. He thought of his dad. His thoughts quickly switched to the girl wondering who she was. He never knew anyone like that in high school.

It would be nice to meet someone like that, he thought.

He wouldn't be able to take her to JP's football games because that was over ten years ago. Could it be that he was already 27 years old? He checked the time on his phone and put it back on the nightstand. He stared at the picture of Brittany, his ex-girlfriend. He meant to move it elsewhere, or get rid of it entirely, but couldn't bring himself to do it.

He looked around his room. It was spotless and sparse, like the rest of his house. He had only what he needed, except for the art that hung on most of the walls. Almost all of it related to the ocean somehow. It added life and color to his otherwise minimalistic home.

Bass rolled out of bed, being careful not to bump his leg. The hospital released him only two days ago and while the abrasions still hurt, they were healing quickly. He hobbled into the bathroom and looked into the mirror. His body was lean and strong. He looked at his stomach and flexed.

"At least that stupid drunk didn't take my abs away," Bass grumbled.

After a quick shower, he put on a new set of bandages and got dressed. He squirted a glob of gel into his thick, dark brown hair and combed it forward, but then tousled it with his hand. Perfectly messy.

He limped carefully downstairs to the kitchen and reached for an apple when he heard his front door open.

"Hey-o!" called JP, walking in with a basket in his hands. He wore his usual workout clothes and backwards ball cap which covered his short blond hair.

"This is for you," he said as he set the basket on the kitchen counter. "It's from everyone at the gym. I know, it's a little late. I didn't even tell them you got hurt until yesterday, so it's on me. Not them."

Bass looked at the basket full of fruit—some protein powder, vitamins, and other items clearly plucked from the gym's store.

A COUNCIL OF ANGELS

Bass picked up the card sporting the gym's logo. Inside, it simply read, "Get Well Soon."

JP helped himself to a banana from the basket. "How's the leg?"

"Bloody."

"Nasty," JP replied with a mouth full of banana.

Bass took a bite of an apple and said, "I woke up this morning with a crazy dream. We were back in high school and I was at one of your games, but I was with a girl. I couldn't see her face, but man, I really liked the feeling I had with her. I can't describe it."

"What did she look like?"

"I don't know. But I really liked her. Like, her energy or something. It felt good. Know what I mean?"

"Hmm… I guess. One day, buddy. You'll meet her."

"My dad was there too."

"Yeah?"

"Yeah."

Just then, the doorbell rang.

"How much you wanna bet it's your mama?" JP said. "No, no," he scolded as he walked to the door, "don't you move your precious little legs, I got it."

JP opened the door. "Well, look who's here! Hi Mom!" He swung the door open, welcoming Kathy in, and yelled over his shoulder to Bass. "Told you so."

"Hi JP, nice to see you," Kathy said. She hugged him as she entered the house.

"Hi Mom," Bass said. Kathy crossed the front room quickly, reaching Bass, who sat on a barstool in the kitchen.

"Hi, honey," she said, looking him over. She gave him a side hug, being careful of his leg. "How are you doing? How's your leg? How's your head?" She put her hand on his forehead.

Bass recoiled slightly and said, "I don't have a temperature, Mom. I'm fine."

"He says he's bloody," JP said, grinning. Kathy didn't think it was funny. Her eyes narrowed on Bass's leg and focused on the new bandages.

"Really, how are you?" she asked.

"Seriously, I'm fine. Watch." Bass walked from the kitchen to the living room and sat down on the couch. It stung when he bent his knee as the scabs threatened to crack open, but he put on his best poker face. He didn't want his mom to worry.

Kathy followed him into the living room.

"I like your hair," JP said, looking at Kathy. "Blond. You can never go wrong with blond."

"Yes, thank you, JP," Kathy said. "I like it because it hides the grays."

"Have you been working out too?"

Kathy laughed. "No, I'm too busy for that. But thank you again. I can see you've put on some muscle though."

JP beamed as he pushed his chest out. "I've added 20 pounds and reduced my body fat by 2%. Now, if I can only grow a couple inches more and beat out your son." JP let out a big sigh. "I suppose Bass will always beat me in the height department, though."

"Yeah, and you'll always beat me in the ghost-white skin department," Bass said.

"You're just jealous of my blue eyes," JP replied.

"And you're jealous of my bronze skin."

"More like salted caramel skin."

"Are you always thinking about food?"

"Pretty much."

Kathy enjoyed the banter as she surveyed the front room.

"You haven't changed things much since I was here last. Are you going to get any roommates?"

"I've told you before, Mom, I don't want or need any roommates. I'm fine."

"Well, are you putting some money away? Are you saving?"

"Yes, mother," Bass sighed.

"That's important, you know. I'm just making sure." Kathy looked out the front window towards the beach. "Still, it seems wrong to have a fancy house so close to the beach and be alone. Do you at least throw some good parties here?"

"Not really. I stay busy with work."

"Yeah," JP interrupted. "Getting hit by a drunk driver was just what he needed to actually take some time off."

Bass rolled his eyes, but JP grinned, proud of his jab.

"When will you be back up my way?" Kathy asked.

"I'm not sure. I mean, maybe if I can make some contacts up there, I can justify the trip. But," Bass glanced at Kathy, "it's pretty much all old people in that whole Monterey area."

"Thanks," Kathy snapped back.

"You know what I mean."

"Yeah. Well, I got a new place and I could use your decorating skills. I like the art you have here. Maybe you could help me?"

"I could just give you some pointers."

JP sat down at the kitchen bar and started on his second banana. He methodically pulled the peel down in thin strips.

"Well, I'd also love to show you some of the work I've done with your dad's family history. I've traced some of his ancestors all the way back to Europe. Did you know you've got royal blood? It's true."

In a flash, Bass thought about his dad. He didn't like it. He deflected it.

"Yeah, I'm sure everyone has a king and queen somewhere in their family history, Mom. It doesn't really make me feel that special. I focus on the here and now. Especially now. I've got to work harder than ever."

Kathy's face fell, but she smiled and tried again.

"Well, it's really neat. Maybe you'll let me show you one of these days?"

"Yeah, sure thing."

Bass looked at the time.

"Well…" he started, "I was going to head into work today. I'm tired of lounging arou—"

"What?" JP bursted out, his mouth full of banana. "You're seriously going into work? But I'm here. I took the day off. And your mom's here."

Bass shot a quick look at Kathy. She raised her eyebrows, awaiting his answer.

"I've got a new line going to production and I want to make sure it's all good to go. I don't know what's happening with that moron at the warehouse." Bass looked at Kathy and said, "I need to go in for at least a few hours, and then we can do something. Is that OK?"

"Yes, of course, honey," Kathy said. "I understand. Am I sleeping in the bedroom down here? I'll put my stuff in there."

"Yeah, sure. That's fine."

Bass looked over at JP, who glared back. He intentionally lifted the banana peel up so Bass could see and then dropped it on the floor.

"If you're well enough to go into work, you're well enough to bend down and pick that up."

"Nice," Bass said.

"No, wait. Crap. Kathy will probably just clean it up."

"Probably," Kathy chimed in.

JP sighed as he bent over to pick up the peel. "Dude, just hurry, OK? I had to cancel a few of my training sessions to be here today. And they were rich Newport ladies."

"And Bass, sweetie, when you get back we can discuss which countries you're going to. You might be able to help me do a bit of research from there."

JP shot Kathy a look.

"Huh? What are you talking about?" Bass asked.

JP, who stood behind Bass, shook his head no and made a

cutting motion at his throat. He mouthed the words, "I haven't told him."

Kathy quickly backtracked. "Oh nothing. If you want to talk about family history and what countries your ancestors are from, just let me know."

Bass sensed something was up, but couldn't figure out what. He spun to look at JP, who had already pulled out his phone and was pretending to text someone.

He glanced back at Kathy and said, "Yeah, sure, Mom. Maybe when I get home we can talk about how kings and queens had babies so that centuries later I could be born."

CHAPTER SIX

Bass opened his garage door and slowly backed his black Range Rover out of the driveway. His motorcycle was still at the shop being repaired but, honestly, he was glad to be up off the ground and behind some airbags.

He pulled out onto Pacific Coast Highway, or PCH, as everyone called it. As he headed down the road, he felt a twinge of guilt about leaving his mom behind at the house. After all, she made the six-hour drive from Monterey to be with him. He looked in the rearview mirror, his brown eyes staring back. *I'll just work fast*, he thought.

Five minutes later, Bass arrived at the warehouse where his office was located, let out a sigh, and said, "It's good to be back at work again."

As he locked his car and headed inside, he was proud of what he'd accomplished. After his first year of college, he took the money he made from selling his high school landscaping business and invested it into a new company. He also dropped out of college and never looked back.

Like many single guys from Orange County, he dreamed of having a surf apparel company. The difference was, Bass actual-

24

ly did it. He studied all the big brands he wished to compete with and after a lot of hard work and a stroke of luck, he partnered with one of the largest apparel manufacturers in Southern California.

The manufacturing company was owned by a 49-year-old woman named Jen. She and her former husband grew their business from a humble silk screening shop to a thriving apparel empire. Jen liked what she saw in Bass and allowed him to use her entire operation. There, he produced his own designs and fulfilled orders under his own brand while Jen got a 30% cut. Within less than six months, he proved he was onto something and sales came pouring in.

That was nine years ago.

Since then, Bass grew the company almost single-handedly. Aside from using Jen's operational resources, he outsourced or contracted practically every other aspect of the business. From designs, to marketing, to sales, it was lean, profitable, and growing fast. His exit plan was to build his company and then eventually sell to a national or even international brand.

After the first year, Jen trusted Bass completely and backed away from the day-to-day operations. He typically only worked with the general manager that ran Jen's principal business. His name was Derrick, but everyone called him Mr. Tight Pants Man. Nobody knew where the name came from, but most people suspected it was Bass. He and Derrick weren't exactly fond of each other, but they both did their jobs well and managed to get things done.

Bass looked at the whiteboard on his office wall. He had a meeting with Mr. Tight Pants Man in five minutes. He grabbed his tablet and headed to the conference room. Haley, the VP of operations for Jen's principal company, showed up first. She set her tablet on the table and smiled.

"Hi Bass, I'm glad to see you."

"Thank you," he said. He liked Haley. She was professional

and always genuine. He appreciated her honesty, especially when she thought he had a bad idea.

"So, you're all good?" she asked, scanning him up and down, looking for some evidence of the accident.

"Yeah, basically a headache that hasn't gone away yet and some cuts on my leg."

"That's so lucky!"

"Yeah, I suppose. Not lucky for the drunk who hit me, though. He's some old guy who probably won't be driving again soon. Good riddance. One less drunk on the road."

Haley shifted a little in her chair.

"I get that Bass. I do. I'm sorry this happened. But hopefully the man that hit you can maybe change his life around? Does he have a family? Will he be able to drive to a job? That kind of thing."

Bass never considered that before. Haley always had a great point of view on things. She was nice, and it had a way of infecting him, making him a nicer person, too.

"What's his name?" she asked.

"I don't even know."

He thought about the guy that hit him when Derrick walked into the conference room. He carried a notepad in one hand and a large coffee mug in the other. He sat down and pulled at his tight khakis to stretch them over his short, chubby legs. He took a loud sip of his coffee, then put the cup down and snorted loudly with his mouth open. He looked like he swallowed something before speaking.

"Hi Bass, glad to see you're back. You had what, like one sick day?"

"It's been a few days but, yeah, I'm here."

Derrick took another loud sip and opened his notes. He glanced at Haley, who waited with her tablet ready. "OK," he said, "straight to the point, we had to delay your new line."

"You what?"

"We," Derrick stressed, "had to delay your new line until you were back. I had to put another line into production to make our dates. We couldn't wait for you to show up."

Bass couldn't believe his ears. He'd already talked up the line to many of the local surf shops and had a lot of purchasers eager to buy.

"I was hit by a freaking drunk driver man," he said. "Not my fault."

"Yeah, I'm sorry about that. But I've got to manage the production around here. Your line will only be delayed a couple of weeks."

Bass clenched his fists. He knew it wasn't another product line. He knew it was Derrick being forgetful or lazy. Or both.

"Is there anyway we can get it into production now?"

"Not at this point, no. I mean, you can reach out to Brittany and see what her team might be able to do."

Bass shifted in his chair and clenched his fists even tighter.

This guy's unreal! he thought. *My ex-girlfriend is none of his business.*

"Not sure if you got the memo, but we broke up a while back. We're not exactly on the best of terms." Bass said. "Besides, her team is better suited for other projects. Not the stuff I'm trying to get done."

"Maybe, maybe not. This might be a good time to partner with her family's company then."

"You have no clue what you're talking about. You've never even dealt with them. I know what kind of work they can handle and it's not what I need."

Derrick took another sip, staring at Bass over the rim of the coffee cup. He adjusted himself again and said, "You know, Bass, I have no doubt you're going to be very successful one day. Look at what you've already done. You have your fancy SUV, your motorcycle, your house by the pier, and so on. But the sad thing is that you won't have anyone in your life to share it with."

"Derrick!" Haley burst out. "Is that really necessary?"

Bass's first instinct was anger, but he knew what was happening. A long time ago, he decided he would outsmart bullies. He smiled and said, "When will the line go into production? I need a date."

Derrick was caught off guard—confused that he hadn't upset Bass. He squinted his eyes, evaluating him, and then he shook his head as if snapping out of a trance. He picked up his pen and glanced down at his notepad and said, "Yeah…we can…um…get it going in three weeks."

"Fine," Bass said. "If we're no longer discussing work issues, we're done here." Bass grabbed his tablet and stood up. He looked at Haley, who shrugged her shoulders and turned her head sideways.

"Sorry," she whispered.

Bass walked towards the door as tall and forceful as he could. He tried his best to hide the fact that his leg burned with each step.

CHAPTER SEVEN

"Hey," Bass texted, "wanna meet at Pancho's?"

JP texted back immediately. "Yeah. I can be there in 5."

"OK. I'm already here."

Bass picked at the tortilla chips while he waited for JP to arrive. With each chip, he carefully squeezed a lime, drenching it with juice, and then poured salt over it. He put the part of the chip with the juice and salt face down on his tongue and slowly crunched, savoring the flavor.

As Bass reached for another chip, the music in the restaurant skipped a beat. He turned around in his chair to see a CD player attempting to provide ambience to the taco shop.

Old school, he thought.

As he spun back around, his left leg hit the table, sending a thousand tiny needles stabbing into his skin. He jammed his eyes shut, sucked in hard through his teeth, and pounded the table with his fist. As the pain seared through his leg, it seemed to writhe its way towards his heart and he realized it wasn't just the scabs on his skin, he was aching inside.

Bass opened his eyes and redirected his thoughts to Brittany. The pain in his leg subsided, but he wondered if there was still a chance. Tempted to call her, he reasoned that she would for sure want to know he was in a car wreck. He opened his phone just as the owner of the restaurant walked up.

"Hola Señor Martinez. Cómo estás?" he asked.

"Hi Pancho. How are you?"

"Why do you not speak to me in Spanish? You have Mexican blood. It's your heritage, you know."

"I'm only half-Mexican," Bass replied without looking up from his chips. "I also have German blood and whatever else my mom is." He wasn't in the mood to be told what he should do. He shot a glance at Pancho's face and quickly changed his tone. "But you're right, I suppose. I will try to learn more."

"Bueno," Pancho said, his face changing back to a smile. "It will be good for you. They say smart people know more than one language. I guess that makes me pretty smart, no?"

Bass gave him a courtesy laugh and shook his head yes.

"OK, Señor Martínez, I will leave you to your food but thank you for always coming here."

"Thank you for having the best tacos in all of Huntington Beach."

Pancho's chest inflated with pride, and he slapped Bass on the back and walked away. Bass's thoughts swirled around as Derrick's last words buzzed in his skull. Derrick was wrong. Bass knew what he was doing. He was doing it faster than anyone else he knew. In fact, if he played his cards right, he'd meet his goals by the end of the year and then he'd have time to focus on starting a family, whatever that meant. He picked up his phone again to text Brittany.

"Can I get you something to drink while you wait?" a voice interrupted.

Bass looked up at the server. She was nice and was the one that always waited on him. He never learned her name.

"No, thanks."

"Yikes! What happened to your leg?"

Bass looked down and realized some blood was seeping out of his bandage, a deep maroon color streaming down his leg. He quickly grabbed a napkin to wipe it up.

"Oh, just had a small accident. That's all."

She lowered her head, raised one eyebrow, and said, "That looks way worse than a small accident." She looked back towards the front door as a couple entered the restaurant. "But OK, let me know if I can get you something."

JP showed up a few minutes later. He sat down and dove into the tortilla chips. Bass noticed his muscled arms covered in veins. Even though JP was an inch shorter than Bass, he was much stronger. Bass figured all that muscle mass was why JP was always eating something.

It was well past lunch hour, and Pancho's Taco Shop was slowing down. There were only a few other customers in the restaurant.

The server returned with a strawberry lemonade and put it in front of JP.

"Thank you, Emma. You always know what I want."

Emma, Bass thought.

"The usual? Five carne asadas?"

"You got it."

She turned to Bass and asked, "What can I get you?"

"Yeah, I'll take the pastor tacos. Four of them. Can you guys leave off the onions this time?"

"No problem. Everything else? Cilantro, pineapple?"

"Yeah, that's great. Thanks."

Emma turned back to the kitchen to place the order.

"Where's my mom? I thought she'd be with you?"

"After you took off to work, she said she was going to rest. Just so you know, she left super early this morning to be here today. Maybe you could be a little nicer to her."

"Dude, I just asked where she is. I don't need any family counseling. I've already gotten enough of that today."

"What do you mean?"

"Never mind."

"I know you, man. Something's not right."

"Dude, I got hit by a freaking drunk driver. Of course it's not right!"

"Nah, that's not what I'm talking about. You've been distancing yourself. You're putting everything into work so you can supposedly cash out or whatever, but I think there's something deeper going on. I'm the only person you hang out with anymore."

JP's words stung. He was getting close to something Bass didn't like to admit, even to himself. He thought of how he was just tempted to text Brittany, and a single thought flashed into his mind—loneliness. He quickly changed the subject.

"Whatever, man. I can tell you're up to something. What is it?"

"I'm just gonna put it out there," JP said. "You and I need to go to Europe and we need to go fast."

The music skipped another beat.

"What?"

"I'm not even gonna try to do a hard sell here. It should be pretty freaking obvious to you, man." JP paused, as though trying to remember some points he'd probably already thought up. "Look, you could have die—"

"Oh brother," Bass interrupted.

"I'm serious, dude! The cop said if that guy had hit you straight on, you'd be dead right now."

"That's not what he said."

"Close enough."

Bass shifted in his seat, getting annoyed. He didn't take vacations. He just lost three days, and it cost him valuable time on getting his new line out.

JP pushed on.

"Instead of thinking about work, you should be thinking

about how freaking precious your life is, man. You could be dead right now! I could be seeing your blood stains every time I drive down Beach Blvd. But you're not dead. You lucked out big time. And I think you should take advantage of this renewed lease on life to do some cool stuff."

Bass scoffed. "Lease on life?"

JP put a handful of chips into his mouth all at once and crunched them down enough to start speaking again. "I've already got an idea for the itinerary. One of my friends at work just got back from a four-week trip around Europe."

"Four weeks! No way, dude."

"I said *he* took four weeks. Not us. You and I are just going for like two weeks or so. We'll knock out some of the coolest parts of Europe. France, Italy, Spain, England, and maybe some other countries. I've got to figure that out."

Bass squirted lime juice onto another chip, salted it, and put it on his tongue. He thought about JP's proposal. He had to admit, he'd always wanted to see Europe. Especially Italy. Everyone always raved about it.

"No," Bass said, shaking his head. "I've got to get my line out. I gotta make sure that happens."

"And when is that happening?"

"In a few weeks from now."

"Isn't everything already kind of done for that? Your designs and stuff? You were talking it up before you were hit. Wasn't it good to go?"

Bass thought about it. All he had to do now was wait. He did actually have time. The music skipped again. It was getting on his nerves. Bass closed his eyes and sighed loudly.

"What?" JP asked.

"Nothing."

"Well, anyway, think about your own parents," JP said. "You lost your dad when you were young and they never got to do anything cool, right?"

Bass opened his eyes, shooting JP a look. It was a sensitive topic for Bass. Knowing he'd gone too far, JP quickly changed the subject.

"Besides, I hear that Italy has the hottest girls and they like California guys."

Bass decided to let JP get away with taking a shot at his parents.

"No," Bass said, "I've heard that English women are the hottest."

"What?" JP practically choked on his chips. "No way, dude. British chicks? No way! Italian women. Or maybe the Spanish. Yeah, probably the Spanish. I don't know. Let's just go find out."

Just then, Emma showed up with two plates full of tacos. She put Bass's plate down first and then smiled at JP as she put his plate down. She stood closer to him than a normal server would. She made eye contact with JP. "Can I get you guys more chips? Maybe some guac?"

"No, I think we're good," Bass answered.

Emma walked away, and Bass looked down at his tacos. He considered actually going to Europe. He then glanced up at JP, who hadn't even started eating. He simply stared at Bass with an eager look on his face. He raised his eyebrows, opened his mouth, and nodded his head yes.

"OK, I'll think about going."

"Umm…about that. I may have already booked some tickets for us."

"What? Are you serious?"

"Oh yeah," JP said, finally taking a bite of his taco, but it was too hot. He blew out quickly and some carne asada launched from his mouth and flew towards Bass and landed behind his chair.

"Just eat your tacos, buddy. You let 'ol JP take care of the rest."

April 9, 6:00 a.m.

Greetings Team,

Thank you all for being willing to work with me. I can't believe that I've been given such an important task for my first assignment. I'll do my best. You know how much this means to me.

I've already seen so much and I have to say, it's been such an overwhelming assignment getting to be with Bass. As instructed, I haven't interacted with him yet and I've tried my best to simply record everything for the report I know I'll have to deliver.

The time is fast approaching and in just one day, we'll get started with Bass. With what I've seen so far, I think we've got our work cut out for us.

What he chooses to do is up to him, but I'm positive we can make a powerful impact. I really hope he'll take us up on the offer. I've learned so much from you already. I'll depend on your skills and insights for a successful outcome. You all have been angels for a lot longer than I have, so I'll follow your lead.

Warm Regards,
   Michael

CHAPTER EIGHT

"You know there's no smoking on the pier, right?"

Bass looked directly at an old, scruffy guy who had a cigarette in one hand while holding a fishing pole in the other. He didn't notice or care that Bass was speaking to him.

Just half an hour before, Haley convinced Bass to take a walk down the pier. They stopped once they got to the end to look out towards Catalina Island. That's when the smell of cigarette smoke filled Bass's nose.

"Hey buddy," Bass said louder and more forcefully, "there's no smoking here. You're going to have to put that out."

The man barely turned and looked at Bass. "Who are you? Some sort of junior cop?"

"Nope, just a healthy citizen who likes to keep the air clean for other people."

Bass fixed his eyes on the guy. It was a showdown, and they both seemed to know. Bass disdained smoking and had very little tolerance for those who smoked in public. He almost always said something to the offending smoker directly.

"Look at the sign right above your head. It says no smoking."

The fisherman didn't look up but shot a quick glance at the

other people taking notice. He wasn't going to back down to some punk kid, but also didn't want to deal with the police or anyone else.

He smashed the cigarette on the pier and flicked it in Bass's direction. Bass took a step closer. "You realize you just littered, right?"

Haley reached for his arm and whispered, "Let it go."

The man turned back to the ocean and adjusted his fishing line. Bass thought about it for a second but dropped it and began walking with Haley back down the pier towards the beach.

"I don't get people like that. If you want to trash your own body that's fine, but why make the rest of us deal with their stupid addiction?"

"What's bothering you today?" Haley asked. He shrugged his shoulders but remained quiet. She was just a few years older than he was, but Bass always thought she was much wiser. He figured it had to do with being a single mom. Being alone with a teenage daughter had to be hard, and he appreciated her for that.

"Really Bass, what's happening?"

Bass ran his hand through his hair. "I think it's the thing with Mr. Tight Pants Man. I can't believe he suggested I contact Brittany. I mean, for starters, he should have put my new line into production first. It was on the books. He should have made it happen. I feel like he did that to spite me."

Haley nodded. "Yeah, maybe."

"I mean, I know Jen likes him, but I don't get how a guy like that made it to where he is. I seriously think he's lazy. Not to toot my own horn or anything but I started my first business when I was twelve."

"Twelve?" Haley asked.

"Yeah. I mean, technically it was a lawn mowing route in my neighborhood. My mom was struggling, and I wanted to have more money. It was around that time, when a 17-year-old guy on my street, bought a new car. I asked him how he did it and he told me he saved his lawn mowing money. I started knocking doors the next day and hustled ever since."

"So, you got started by mowing lawns and then that somehow turned into apparel?"

"Yeah," Bass said, "I branched out to include other landscaping services. I hired some guys that did all the work for me while I was at school. I handled the money with the clients and driving new business."

Bass paused as he thought about his mom. She was the one who actually bought him his first lawnmower. A day after telling her he was going to mow lawns to make money, he came home from school to a shiny new lawnmower with a bow on it. A note read:

To my handsome young entrepreneur—I hope this helps you get started!

Love you,
Mom

A couple years later, she also introduced him to a neighbor who helped set him up as an actual business. He felt a sudden twinge of guilt for not spending more time with her recently. She only stayed two days before having to go back to work.

"And then what happened?" Haley asked.

"Huh? Oh, yeah, I grew the business and then sold it after my first year at college."

"So you really have done everything on your own. It's impressive, Bass. You should feel proud of what you've done."

Bass nodded. It was good to see that at least someone else respected his work.

Haley continued. "Do you miss having a business like your landscaping one? You ran a company while you sat through biology class. Now you're so busy. Wouldn't you like to go back to that? Being less busy, I mean?"

"That's not the point," Bass said. "I'm working super hard now so I don't have to be busy ever again."

"We'll see if that happens," Haley said. "I know a lot of hardcore entrepreneurs like you who can't wind down. They keep going on to the next thing."

"Well, that's not me. I'll be ready to do the family thing and travel more."

"Yeah, I get that."

They walked in silence for just a minute before Haley said, "Bass, I hate to ask this, but do you think there's still something there with Brittany?"

Hearing Brittany's name from someone else always struck a nerve. Honestly, Bass wanted there to be a happy fairytale ending with her, but he had no clue. He looked down the pier and saw a couple holding hands. They both wore workout clothes, and he instantly remembered the day he first met Brittany.

It was at a gym where JP used to work and Bass had joined JP for lunch. From JP's desk, he could see everyone who came into the gym. The doors opened and Brittany walked in, her tight-fitting gym clothes leaving little to the imagination. Bass immediately liked what he saw and said to JP, "Watch and learn, amigo."

He walked up to Brittany and said, "Tacos?"

"What?" she replied.

"Tomorrow night. Dinner. Tacos. I just need your address to come pick you up."

Brittany looked at him for a moment. She then scanned him up and down, like a boxer evaluating her next opponent. Bass kept his eyes fixed on hers.

"Smooth," she said, nodding approvingly. "Let's see if you can back it up." She smiled and gave him her number.

Not wanting to ruin the moment, Bass turned around and

headed for the door, walking as tall as he could. As he passed JP, he mouthed the words, "Holy crap, it worked!"

JP whispered back. "You left your lunch here. I'm going to eat it."

After their first date, things moved fast. They had a lot in common. Bass learned that Brittany was just as driven as he was, if not more so. She worked for her family business, which, ironically, was also a clothing manufacturer. It was the largest operation in California and shipped apparel worldwide. It was different enough from Bass's own line that they weren't in direct competition.

Romantically, Brittany was the closest Bass came to loving someone. After five months of dating, he told her. One night, after a nice dinner, they took a walk on the beach. He stopped her, gave her a kiss, and whispered, "I love you."

She leaned back and said, "Really?"

A dark pit opened up inside him and he immediately felt dumb for saying it. He hated feeling so vulnerable and exposed. After that, it got weird, and she ended it not long after. He got busy with work and tried to forget about dating. That was over six months ago. They saw each other randomly, but it was always awkward, at least for him.

"Bass," Haley asked again, "do you think there's still a chance with Brittany?"

Haley's voice brought him back to the present. "Huh? What? I mean, no. I don't think so."

"What about professionally? Her company probably would love to get their hands on a brand like yours."

Bass never really considered that. Brittany was not competition, so he never thought about her company as a possible buyer.

As they arrived at the entrance of the pier, something caught Bass's eyes on the steps to the beach along the north side of the pier. Three skaters scooped up sand and snickered quietly to themselves as they shot glances towards a man who sipped from a cup of coffee. Bass looked closer and saw the man's cane folded at his side. He was blind. Bass looked back at the guys and realized what they were up to.

"Hold on," Bass said. "Check that out. Something's up."

Sure enough, the guys walked quietly towards the blind man. Bass ran off the pier and onto the steps while the guy in front was trying to keep the sand from falling out of his hand.

"Hey!" Bass yelled, but it was too late. They threw the sand in the blind man's cup and took off running. Bass ran up and without asking, grabbed the cup from the blind man. The man let out a gasp and recoiled backwards.

"Sir, I'm sorry to grab the coffee out of your hand like that, but some punks just put sand in it. I didn't want you to drink it."

The blind man moved his head back and forth, using his ears to figure out what was happening. Bass saw the man's hearing aids and leaned in closer to explain louder what happened.

Haley took the man's hand and asked if they could get him another cup of coffee.

The man smiled at the sound of her voice. "That would be nice. Thank you." His voice was raspy, like he hadn't spoken in a while.

He turned towards Bass and reached out to shake his hand. Then the man moved his hand up along Bass's arm to his face. Feeling self-conscious, Bass shifted his eyes around, looking to see who might be watching.

"We'll be right back with your coffee," Bass said loudly.

"Thank you. Thank you."

Bass glanced at Haley, who smiled.

"Stay right here OK, sir? We'll be right back."

Haley and Bass walked towards the coffee shop across the street.

"Dude, I can't even believe those guys!" Bass said. "If there's such a thing as a hell, those guys are for sure going there. Seriously, putting sand in a blind man's cup of coffee? Freaking idiots."

Haley smiled and said, "Well, at least it allows us to get in a good deed for the day. That was pretty cool of you, by the way."

They stood on the sidewalk, waiting to cross. As the light turned, they stepped into the road just as a lady in a minivan zoomed past, running the red light. She just barely missed hitting them. They stared at the car as it drove past. It had a bumper sticker that said, "Angels are all around."

"That's pretty ironic," Haley said.

"Yeah, she's going to need some angels with the way she's driving!"

CHAPTER NINE

At this point, I just have to say, I'm really excited to share this with you. I've tried to make this report somewhat official so far and have kept my own observations to a minimum. This was the first time though that Bass got to see us. I have to admit, emotionally speaking, it was a little overwhelming. Thankfully, the council prepared me for this.

It was the day after the walk with Haley that Bass set out to surf about an hour before sunrise. He threw his wetsuit on up to his waist, being careful of his leg, grabbed his shortboard and left through the garage's side door.

It was his first time getting back into the ocean since the accident. He hustled down the path that ran between the beach and PCH, checking out the waves as he went. Even in the predawn light, he could see the sets were shoulder-high and breaking right, his favorite. Best of all, the beach was empty, and he loved knowing that he would have the waves to himself.

Bass ran down the steps and plowed his toes into the cold sand. He put his board down and reached behind to pull up the zipper of his wetsuit. Spinning his arms like a windmill, he loosened up the suit to get the perfect fit. As he widened his stance, he grimaced as he felt a brief twinge from his leg. The road rash was still healing.

He inhaled, filling his lungs with the salty air. This was one of his favorite things to do. In fact, it was one of the few things that slowed him down. With his pre-surfing ritual complete, he reached down and strapped the surfboard's leash to his ankle, lifted the board, and trotted towards the waves.

Before he knew what happened, he saw a bright light and got knocked backwards. He teetered for just a second and then fell flat on the sand into a sitting position. He tried to stand, but stumbled. When he tried to walk forward, he saw another light and got knocked backwards again. This happened a third time. He closed his eyes, rubbed them, and took a few deep breaths, trying to fight off feelings of dizziness.

When he opened his eyes, he saw three people standing a few feet away from him. Their clothes were bright white, and they seemed to glow in the early morning light. They were so bright, in fact, that Bass put his hand up to shield his eyes.

As he looked closer, he could see two women and one man. The guy was big. He wore a white three-piece suit and a ridiculously huge silver watch. He was bald and his head glowed brightly in the predawn light.

Next to him was a woman who wore white flowing pants with a loose white blouse. She had long, charcoal-black hair, kept back by a light blue bandana.

Next to her was the other woman who wore what looked like an all-white 1950s poodle skirt. It had a red poodle on it that matched her red belt and the red scarf she had tied around her neck. But it was her bright orange curly hair that really stood out. It seemed to explode out of her head. When she saw Bass, she covered her mouth with both hands and giggled.

For the first time since starting my work with Bass, I felt myself becoming visible, and I appeared next to him. I was wearing white pants and white flip-flops with a white-collared shirt, open at the top.

Bass focused on my flip-flops and then slowly gazed upwards to my face. He shook his head back and forth, rubbed his eyes, and massaged his temples, thinking he was having some kind of dream. I watched him bite hard on the inside of his cheek and wince at the pain.

The redhead looked at me and then back at Bass.

"This is so great," she said. She practically laughed when she spoke. "Let's do a proper introduction," she said, and pointed to the black-haired angel. "This is Mary. She's your spiritual angel. The big guy is Jacob."

Jacob put a hand on his chest and took a bow.

"He's your physical angel." Then she pointed at me and said, "The guy next to you with the lovely mop of dark hair is Michael. He's your...umm, guys, what are we calling Michael?"

"He's the secretary angel," Jacob said.

The redhead laughed. "I think the term is 'administrative professional', Jacob. Well, whatever he is, he's a swell guy." She leaned in closer to Bass and whispered, "He's a newbie, so go easy on him, will ya?"

Bass looked at me. "Your name is seriously Michael? An angel named Michael...isn't that a little cliché?"

I nodded and smiled, admitting he was right.

Bass looked back to the redhead and asked, "And what's your name?"

She spun around on one foot, twisting her skirt into the air, opened her arms wide and said, "I am Rebekah." She took a bow and said, "I am your relationship angel. But most people call me the love angel."

"No, they don't," Jacob said quickly.

"Yes, they do," Rebekah shot back as she spun again and landed a finger on Jacob's chest. "You're just jealous because all you do is talk about boring physical stuff. I get the good stuff!"

She spun back to look at Bass, lowered her voice a little, and said, "Like how to woo a girl."

Mary smiled, but had a more serious tone when she spoke.

"Sebastian," she said, "the four of us, Jacob, Rebekah, Michael, and myself, are your council of angels, and we've been assigned to work with you. We've been waiting for you to take a step in the right direction. Helping a blind man yesterday was exactly what we needed."

She paused to give Bass time to process his thoughts. As sharp as he was, I could tell he was thrown off. He remained sitting in the sand, staring up at us, a blank look on his face.

Mary continued. "We're assigned to work with you for 40 days and it begins the day you accept our help. If you do, our job is to help you find your life's greatest treasure. If you're willing to work with us, we promise we'll do all that we can to help you find it."

Everyone stood still except Rebekah, who rocked back and forth on her legs, almost dancing. She kept staring back and forth between Bass and me. Everyone waited for Bass to speak next.

He sat forward, wincing as his leg stung. It brought him back to reality. "OK, look, this is fun and all, but I think I'm just having a dream. I'm going to wake up soon and I'm going to realize that I'm at home in bed and I'm going to forget all about this—just like I forget most of my dreams."

"Bass," I jumped in and said, "this is really happening. We're angels on assignment to help you. But it's got to be your choice. We can only invite. It needs to be your decision."

I could tell he was thinking it over.

"So, if I say yes, all of you are going to help me find gold or something?"

"Not gold. Something infinitely more valuable than gold," Mary said.

"Why can't you just tell me what the treasure is?"

"Oh Bassy, what would be the fun in that?" Rebekah said. "It's a journey. This is the beginning of your story! This is the part where you decide if you're going to be a conquering hero or not."

"I wouldn't put it quite like that," Mary said, "but she's right."

"OK, sport," Jacob said. His voice was deep and direct. "Enough talk. We gotta go. You think about this. We'll be in touch."

As soon as he said that, Jacob disappeared. Mary disappeared as well. Rebekah giggled and jumped up into the air, disappearing as she did so.

My assignment was to remain with Bass to record everything. I remained visible for just a second longer, smiling at him. I faded before his eyes but lingered, watching and observing.

He fell backward onto the sand and looked up to the sky, which was already much lighter. He glanced at the ocean, but his heart sank as he saw some surfers already taking *his* waves. He moved to stand up but fell backward. This time, everything went dark.

The next thing he heard was a garbled sound coming from above him.

"Hey man...hey," a voice said. "Hey man, are you OK?"

Bass opened his eyes. The light was practically blinding. He put his hand up to block the sun and saw a lifeguard standing over him.

"Are you OK? You good?"

"Yeah, I'm good. Must have fallen asleep." Bass looked around. The sun was already well into the sky.

"What time is it?"

The lifeguard checked his watch. "It's 9:43."

"Crap," Bass said. "I've already wasted half my morning. I've got to get to work."

CHAPTER TEN

"Dude, why do you have this here?"

Bass sat at a desk inside the gym where JP worked. It was the day after he had—what he thought was—a crazy dream about angels. He held a photo of a group of friends including JP, himself, and his ex-girlfriend Brittany. His eyes lingered on her— her dark hair, olive skin, impressive figure.

JP watched Bass stare at the photo for a moment and then finally spoke. "You're still hung up on her, aren't you?"

"What? No," Bass said, tossing the photo down on the desk. He knew JP knew he was lying. "I mean, yeah, but whatever. What am I going to do? She ended it. It's kind of good anyway, I guess."

"Yeah, you're building your empire and she's busy building hers. You guys don't have room for each other. Besides, neither of you is really the touchy-feely type, right? You barely even talk to your mom."

"Seriously? That's what you think?"

"Uh, yeah."

Normally Bass would have gone off on anyone who said

something like that, but JP knew him better than anyone else. And he was right. Bass hung his head, feeling guilty again for not spending more time with his mom when she was in town right after his accident. He would make it up. He would go see her.

JP snapped his fingers in front of Bass's face. "Hey, tough guy, are you here today? What's the deal?"

Bass nodded his head. "Yeah, let's work out."

"Well, today was *supposed* to be a leg day, but I'll give you a pass until your leg heals up. It wouldn't be too fun cracking a scab open with every squat I make you do."

"Right, thanks for that."

Bass and JP moved to the bench press and lifted the weights onto both sides of the bar. Bass laid down, gripped the bar, and did a set of 10 to warm up. After the set, he popped up and glanced at himself in the mirror. He looked at JP and asked, "Do you think there's some sort of treasure in life?"

"What do you mean?"

Bass tried to put into words what he understood from the day before. The angels told him they could help him find his life's greatest treasure. Still thinking it was a dream, he thought it might be a sign that he could sell his company and then travel, start a family, and do all that kind of stuff.

"I mean, if you had to name the one thing that's the most important to you, what would it be?"

"Dude, I want a woman in my life. Why do you think we're going to Europe?"

"Huh?"

"I told you it's because life is short and whatever. Really though," JP looked around to make sure nobody was eavesdropping, "I wanna meet someone. I'm ready. And I think you are too."

"And you think I'm gonna find that special someone in Europe, do you?"

"Yeah, in Italy. Or France. She's waiting there for you, buddy. I got a feeling."

"Dude, we live in Huntington Beach, California, home to hundreds of gorgeous single ladies."

"Yeah? Well, get busy finding one."

"Right, and you want me to find a girl in Europe. I don't even know French or Italian or whatever. How could I possibly even talk to a girl there?"

JP smiled. "Love conquers all, my friend. Love conquers all."

Bass laughed and laid back down on the bench to crank out another set. He caught a pretty girl staring down at him as she walked past. She smiled, but kept walking.

"Don't even think about it," JP said. "I know her. She's crazier than Brittany. Besides, do you really want to meet another girl in a gym? It was cheesy the first time you did it."

"Yeah, but she's here. She really exists. Not some fantasy girl from Italy."

"OK, tough guy. We need to add more weight. Then do two more sets."

Bass moved through the rest of his workout with JP coaching him. JP was good at his job. He was a people person and had a lot of friends but always stayed loyal to Bass. One time Bass got in a fight with a wrestler his senior year of high school and the guy hit Bass in the face. The punch caught him off guard and it sent him to the ground right in front of several other students, including a girl Bass liked.

JP caught up to the scene and saw Bass on the ground, holding his face. JP took one look at the wrestler, and although JP was smaller, he charged full force at him, slamming him against the lockers. Just then, a teacher came and broke it up. Bass was humiliated, especially because the other guy gloated about it. "That's what I thought!" he taunted.

JP lifted Bass up and got him out of there before the principal showed up.

A COUNCIL OF ANGELS

Later that week, Bass recognized the wrestler's car in a grocery store parking lot with his surfboard tied to the rack on top. Looking around to make sure nobody would see him, Bass smashed the board with his elbow, breaking it in half. JP was there also, but never told anyone.

After the workout, JP walked Bass to the front of the gym.

"Here's a fun question for you," Bass said. "Do you think there's a point to this life?"

"Whoa, philosophical boy. I was wondering when you'd show up." JP said, laughing at his own joke.

"Really though, if there's some kind of treasure in this life, what do you think it is?"

JP rubbed his chin. "Treasure? I don't know. Get married, have kids, be a good person, grow old and die?"

Bass shook his head and looked down.

"No, there's got to be more than that. Otherwise, I know I'm already on the right track. I just gotta keep working hard until I cash out, and then I don't care what I do. Maybe I'll work at a soup kitchen or something."

"Dude, you can work in a soup kitchen right now. You don't have to wait until you're rich."

"No, thank you. I've got to be 100% focused. Most people aren't, which is why most people aren't as successful as I am by my age."

JP pretended to cough. "Ego!"

"Hey, it's just the truth. Anyway, thanks for the workout. I appreciate it."

"Have you packed yet?"

"No. We don't even leave for another week."

"Yeah, well, I'm packed. I'm going super minimalist style. I've read that European chicks are turned off by seeing dudes walking around with giant backpacks."

"Yeah, exactly," Bass said. "I'm not backpacking around like some smelly hippie."

"Neither am I," JP said. "I'm bringing a small, cool backpack. Anyway, get excited. Get very excited. Those European ladies are about to get a little treat from Orange County."

"Right," Bass said. "Later player."

CHAPTER ELEVEN

As I continue with this report, I still don't entirely understand how I was able to be present for everything that happened with Bass. This is one of those strange times where I ended up in the middle of the waves, watching and recording his words and actions.

In fact, it was after a solid day of work that Bass set out for an afternoon surf session before dinner. Just the day before, he asked JP about finding his life's treasure and the thought kept swimming around in his mind. He wondered what it could be, and he wanted to clear his head by getting into the ocean.

Part of him also wondered if he could surf because his leg still hurt whenever he bent it. And his last attempt at surfing was interrupted by what he thought was an intensely vivid dream while passed out. He didn't even get to surf that day.

Although it was afternoon, the waves were still coming in nice sets about shoulder high. Bass paddled out and got through the first set of waves. He was on the north side of the pier in his favorite spot. He didn't mind showing off for the people watching from the pier. In fact, he thought it helped him do better.

There were about twenty other surfers spread out in what Bass called the "sweet spot." He knew most of them by face and a few by name. He nodded to a few guys and turned his board to check out the incoming waves.

He noticed a bald guy paddle up next to him. He was on a longboard which was all white except for a green turtle graphic in the middle. Bass realized it was the big angel from his dream, or at least, what he thought was a dream.

"It's a good day to be alive," Jacob said to Bass. Bass nodded, but said nothing back. He didn't really enjoy talking to other surfers. Even worse, he didn't want to be seen talking to someone who wasn't really there. Pretending he was watching the waves, Bass casually, but quickly, paddled away.

Jacob followed. "Yeah, I just got this new longboard and I've been anxious to take it for a spin. Today seemed like a good day. You ride longboards at all?"

"No, I only ride shortboards," Bass replied. "Longboards are for old men."

Jacob brushed the comment off with a chuckle. "For me, it's all about feeling the wave, being one with it. You shortboard guys are just trying to do your little tricks but you never really become part of the ocean."

Bass wasn't in the mood and paddled faster, away from the pier. He got to a spot where he was alone and waited for the next set of waves. He looked back to see Jacob not too far behind. He watched as Jacob put his hands in the water, bow his head, and mutter something under his breath.

Just then, Bass looked past Jacob to see a huge wave coming at him fast. He paddled hard to get into position, but it was too late. He got knocked off his board by the oncoming force. His body tumbled through the violent water. He expected to surface but didn't. His leg stung as the scabs cracked open and his lungs burned. He kicked hard, but he didn't know which way was up.

He let go and allowed his body to go limp and suddenly

surfaced. He took a huge breath but panicked to see another huge wave bear down right onto him. Again, Bass was tossed around. He felt a pull on his ankle as his board tugged on its leash in the current. He opened his eyes but only saw green mixed with white foam and sand. Finally, he surfaced again.

He barely had time to take a breath before being hit by yet another huge wave. This one lasted the longest. Bass panicked as the force pushed the air from his lungs. The water pummeled him. His body twisted and shook like a rag-doll in the mouth of a Rottweiler. He had no idea which way was up. He kicked blindly. It started to go dark when he popped up to the surface. He coughed and then choked for air.

His eyes darted around to get his bearings, and he was relieved to see no other waves coming at him. The ocean hissed as the white, frothy bubbles foamed all around him.

Bass pulled his board towards him and got on top, exhausted. He coughed to get the water out of his sinuses. He looked towards the pier and was a good hundred yards away. He rested his head on his board to catch his breath.

"It's a good day to be alive, isn't it?" a voice said.

Bass looked up to see Jacob next to him. He sat on his long-board smiling, seemingly untouched from the recent set of monster waves. Bass looked down at his fingers, which now seemed more like hooks as they clung to his surfboard. He released his grip and slowly looked back up at Jacob.

"Did you do that?"

Jacob's smile got even bigger.

Bass started to speak, but more water forced its way out of his lungs. He coughed again and looked back at Jacob, wondering if he was repeating the same dream. He splashed water on his face, but Jacob was still there.

"Don't worry. Your head is fine. It's all real."

Bass sat up on his board and checked the horizon. A lot of big sets were coming in, but they were out past the break, in a safe spot.

"So that wasn't a dream?"

"Nope."

Bass paused, not wanting to say what he was thinking, but his curiosity got the better of him. "So, angels are real?"

"Of course they are, chief."

"So does that mean that, you know, God is real, too?"

"You really believe all of this was some kind of accident?"

Jacob moved his hands directly over the surface of the water. His eyes seemed to shimmer in the water's reflection.

"OK, wait. I have about a million questions then."

"You're going to have to wait on those, sport. I've got something to tell you and then I gotta go."

"What do you mean?"

"What happened the other day is real. I'm part of a team, a council of angels assigned to you. It's a special gift. You've been given the chance to do something fantastic, to change your life for the better, but you've got to make some big changes. That's why we're here."

"What kind of changes?"

"I'm probably jumping the gun on this one, and it's probably more Mary's kind of thing to say than mine," Jacob said as he looked around and then back at Bass. "Straight up, the key to making this whole thing work is to look outwards, to serve others. In fact, happiness comes to those who serve. You got that? It's really all you need to know."

Bass stared at his surfboard, processing what Jacob said.

"Look, we're here for you. We're on your team, champ. But you've got to choose. It's on you. You're the boss here. You've got to make the decision. We will do all we can in our power to help you. And keep in mind, we *are* angels."

Jacob looked over at the waves coming in near the pier. Bass followed his gaze. There was now a large group of people watching the sets come in. The waves pounded the pier, sending spray up to where everyone stood.

"Your job is to start looking outward. Think about others. If you do, it will change your life. If you don't, it will also change your life, but for the worse." Jacob paused. "I better not say anymore. I'm getting into what Mary has prepared for you."

"Even if I do whatever you guys want me to do, how does this work? Are you gonna randomly show up in my life whenever you want?"

"Ha! Don't worry about that," Jacob said. "All you have to do is think it and we'll be there. Although one of us is almost always there." Jacob looked at me, even though he knew it wasn't my time.

Bass scrunched his face. "What?"

"Never mind," Jacob said. "We each have different roles but we're all working for you." He began paddling his longboard towards the breaking waves.

"And just a little pointer—be nice to the new guy, Michael. This is his first assignment as an angel but I think you're going to like him."

"OK."

"So, you wanna ride another monster wave?"

"I didn't even get to ride the last one. I just got pummeled."

"I'll take that as a yes. Get ready!" Jacob put his hands in the water, closed his eyes, and spoke reverently. "We are grateful for your beauty. Please, show us your power." He opened one eye and peeked at Bass. "But please, something that this guy can handle." He gave Bass a wink.

Just then, the water receded, and Bass saw another wave forming. This time, he paddled quickly to get into position. At the last minute, he turned his board and paddled hard towards the shore. Before he knew it, he was being lifted on the face of the wave. He got to his feet and carved.

The wave formed a glassy green pipeline around him. He bent

down and touched the face of the wave with his hand. His skin felt electrified by the water. Then, somehow, the wave opened back up again. Bass shot a glance behind him to see Jacob, who was riding the nose of his longboard with his eyes closed and arms straight out.

"Show off!" Bass yelled. Jacob laughed. As he did so, he disappeared into the wave. Bass turned back and saw the beach coming towards him fast.

No way can this wave still be so big! he thought.

As if it heard him, the wave became smaller and lost power. The face he was riding quickly faded away, leaving Bass on the crest of a now tiny wave. He cut back a few times, and then got down on his board, and realized the water was only a foot deep. After walking into shore, he turned back and looked at the waves. There was no sign of Jacob or his glowing white longboard.

Bass clapped his hands together and made a bow of respect towards the ocean. It felt like the right thing to do for what was the best wave he'd ever ridden in his life.

CHAPTER TWELVE

Bass looked at the price of the backpack again. It fit well and it was a cool design. Now, he had to decide if it was worth the $189 price tag. He was at a local outdoor retailer where JP told him to get his stuff for the upcoming trip. An older lady wearing a green vest walked by and asked if he needed help. Bass smiled, but shook his head no.

"Do you like it?" another woman asked.

"Yes, but I don't need any he—," Bass turned to see Mary standing behind him, wearing the same white clothing as before. She still wore the light blue bandana in her hair, like something from the 70s.

"I think it's an excellent choice, and it is your favorite color," she said.

"Can anyone else see you?" Bass whispered.

"No, they can't," Mary said.

Bass quickly glanced around, not wanting to look like a crazy person. And he certainly didn't want to be seen with some hippie-looking lady wearing long white robes.

"And how do you know my favorite color?"

"I know pretty much all there is to know about you, Sebast-

59

ian. And for the record, light blue is my favorite color too." She pointed to the bandana in her hair. "I understand you had quite a ride with Jacob yesterday?"

"Yeah, but hold on." Bass took out his phone and put his headphones on. "If I'm going to have a conversation with someone other people can't see, at least I'm going to try to look like I'm not crazy. Am I going crazy? Would you even tell me if I were?"

"No, Sebastian, you're not crazy. I'm part of your council and I'm just as real as you."

A flood of questions poured into Bass's mind, but he didn't want to stand in the middle of a store talking on his phone. "Can you hold on just one minute?"

Mary nodded.

He hurried to the front of the store, bought the backpack, and headed out to the main plaza of the outdoor shopping mall. Mary walked quietly with him the entire time.

"OK, so you're seriously an angel? Like, from God?"

"Yes."

"What was your name again?"

"Mary."

"Where are your wings? Where's your halo?"

"We don't have wings. How we move in and through matter doesn't require something like wings. As for our halo, well, that legend comes from the light that we can sometimes emit. Did you see Jacob's bald head? That can get pretty hard to look at if it catches the sun just right." She chuckled to herself.

"But really, can I, you know, touch you?"

Mary held out her hand. Bass tried to shake it, but felt nothing.

"What you don't feel is my spirit. It's matter but not on a level you can feel or sense in your current state."

"You mean, you're dead or something?"

"Do I look dead?"

"Well, no. I mean, you don't have a physical body or whatever?"

"You mean a body made up of crude elements like yours?"

Something about the way Mary spoke put Bass in his place, but he didn't feel like she was trying to be mean in any way. Just the opposite, actually. Somehow, he felt she truly loved him but, like a good teacher, was waiting for him to piece everything together. Bass moved to a bench and sat down. She sat next to him.

"OK, so your body is made up of spirit or whatever and you can move around however you want and other people can't see you, but I can. Is that correct?"

"That's correct."

"And I can't touch you?"

"Not in your current state, no."

"Where do you live? Like, when you're not with me, where do you go?"

"I'm more than happy to answer your questions, Sebastian, but right now, we're waiting for your decision. Will you accept our help or not?"

"You're talking about the whole treasure thing, right?"

Mary nodded.

"Yeah, I don't know."

Mary scooted a little closer on the bench. "What happened yesterday?"

"You mean surfing with Jacob?"

"Yes."

"I got destroyed by a set of waves."

"After that."

"I saw that Jacob could control the ocean, somehow, and mess with me. Is that what you mean?"

"Yes, that was just a sample of what we're able to do. Our only goal is to help you."

"Why?"

"Because we want you to be happy—plain and simple."

"I am happy," Bass said.

Mary tilted her head down and stared into Bass's eyes. A feeling rocketed into Bass's mind. He instantly felt his own loneliness, and it seemed like Mary could see it, too. He quickly changed the subject.

"Does everyone have a team of angels?"

"Yes, at various points in their life, yes they do. As always though, it's up to every person to choose whether they will accept the help."

"OK, so if everyone has a bunch of angels helping them, why is the world so messed up? Why aren't there more happy people?"

"An excellent question, but first, remember that negativity usually gets more attention than positivity. If you look for it, there's just as much good happening in the world, if not more so. But I did answer your question."

Bass furrowed his eyebrows and looked down, confused.

"People need to accept the help, Sebastian."

"Why? Why not just help? Do it for us?"

"There are a lot of things we can do, but most of what we do is never at the expense of someone's own personal choice. We've been given permission to appear to you and be somewhat dramatic in the hopes that you'll say yes."

"Why?"

"Just look around at the people here, Sebastian. Really look and think about each one."

Bass glanced around at the people in the plaza. Passing by him was a young mother pushing a stroller. Behind her at a table were four teenagers, all of them looking at their phones. Next to them at another table was a bald, middle-aged man reading and making notes in a book. Behind him was a man in torn clothing, sifting through a garbage can for bottles.

Bass looked to the fountain, where a few kids ran in and out

A COUNCIL OF ANGELS

of the water. Their mothers, all wearing yoga pants, sat off to the side in the shade. Bass saw a brunette woman enjoying some frozen yogurt. She closed her eyes and savored each bite.

"OK, so…what? What am I supposed to be looking at?"

"First, how many times do you really stop to observe people? And second, and this is much more important, how many times do you really try to understand them?"

Bass was scared to say what his answer really was—hardly ever.

"Why does that matter?"

"Because, Sebastian, this life is all about serving people. Our goal, as your council, is to help you find your treasure. To do that, you're going to have to look outward."

"OK, really, why can't you just tell me what my treasure is? Why the mystery?"

"I could certainly tell you what it is, but it's quite another experience to actually live it. And that's the point. If you look at these people, many of them have actually met with their own angels. Some of them have moved on to live happier lives. Others, not so much."

"What do you mean? If I don't do whatever I need to do with you guys, I'm going to be some miserable kind of loser or something?"

"I'm not sure of your future, Sebastian, but I can tell you of the people that chose not to work with their angels, they were left with an ever-present feeling that their life is much, much less than what it could have been. It's an incredibly frustrated life and sadly, one that many people are living."

"Why is that? Can't they just remember the angels? Can't they just say, 'hey, angels, I'm ready now' or something like that?"

"When you choose not to work with your angels, you forget about them."

"What about the people that *did* work with their angels? Why

63

aren't they blogging about it or doing movies or writing books or whatever?"

"If you choose to work with us, you'll find your own answer to that. But I will say this, Rebekah was right, this is the beginning of your story."

"So if I don't do whatever I'm supposed to do with you guys, I'm going to live the rest of my life forever frustrated and unhappy? That doesn't seem that bad. I mean, there are people out there killing each other and doing really awful stuff."

"Why do you think that is Sebastian?"

Bass thought about it for a moment. "I don't know," he said, "just dumb people making dumb choices I guess."

"Sebastian," Mary continued, "a lot of people are living in a lot of unnecessary pain. They don't have to be. In many cases, it's self-inflicted through their own negative choices. We want to help you rise above that."

Bass shook his head. "I'm not following."

Mary moved closer and held her hand in front of his eyes and said, "Look."

Bass looked forward and saw the brunette woman eating frozen yogurt. Instead of blocking his view, somehow through Mary's hand, Bass could see everything.

In an instant, he saw the woman's life. She was married to a loving husband with three beautiful children. Every morning, after dropping her kids off at school, she spent two hours serving at a local shelter for women. More images flashed through Bass's mind. They sped up until he was sharing her emotions—laughter, peace, admiration, joy, love.

Mary pulled her hands away. "What did you see?"

"So many things," Bass said, having difficulty describing it.

"Now look," Mary said as she put her hand in front of his eyes again. He looked at the middle-age bald man. Bass instantly felt his worry. It was more than worry. It was fear. Desperation. Regret. He was racing through legal documents. In an instant,

Bass saw the man's workplace. He saw the man pursuing a young woman and knew she wasn't the man's wife. It sped up. He saw the man's wife crying as she packed suitcases. The man watched as she drove off. Bass saw the man losing his house. Next, he was in court. His wife sat opposite of him. The man's life was falling apart.

"Had enough?"

"Yes," Bass said. He looked over again at the man. He both hated and pitied him at the same time.

How could someone be so weak? Bass wondered.

"He had a chance, but he refused to accept the offer. Had his council been able to help him, he wouldn't be going through what he is now."

"And let me guess," Bass said, "the woman eating frozen yogurt worked with her angels?"

Mary nodded.

Bass kicked a rock by his foot and then rubbed at the back of his neck. He didn't like being backed into a corner. It seemed to violate his independence.

"I basically have no choice then," he said. "I either work with you guys to find some kind of treasure thing, or I live a sucky life forever and ever."

Mary spoke softly, but deliberately. "You always have a choice, Sebastian. You're either bettering yourself or you're not. We want to help you find happiness."

"So I have to choose between good and evil or something? Sorry, but no. You can tell God or the universe or whoever, this is too much. This is way too churchy for my taste."

Mary continued, "Sebastian, I'm going to be very direct." Her eyes bored into his. "Did you know that you're living far below your ability? There's so much more you're capable and worthy of. You don't know it, but we do. We hope to help you find it. So in a way, yes, it's choosing good, but it's for your *own* good."

She let the words sit for a moment. Then she said, "We're not your boss. We're your council and we can only guide you. I know how hard you work. Now it's time to work on yourself."

Her words penetrated Bass's heart. He easily could have resented them. He thought he was doing all right for himself. Most other 27-year-olds he knew didn't have the house he did or the business he did. As he thought more though, in a place he didn't want to admit, he knew she was right. There was something missing from his life. He didn't know what, but he was willing to learn. He looked up at her.

"That's what we're hoping for." She smiled and faded from view.

CHAPTER THIRTEEN

Skylar looked at her calendar. It was April 13th. She looked back at her laptop. Her left hand rested on the touchpad, the arrow hovering temptingly above the buy button. She took a deep breath and exhaled.

She stood up and walked to the mirror in her bathroom. She took a clip out of her strawberry blond hair, let it fall, and ran her fingers through it to give it more volume. She leaned in to look into her eyes. Red veins zig zagged closer and closer to her green pupils. She needed to take her contacts out.

She looked up to a pink sticky note on the mirror. It said, "Carpe Diem" with two big underlines. Her eyes refocused in the mirror on her laptop sitting on the desk behind her. The screen showed a round-trip ticket to London. It was leaving in one day. She would barely have enough time to pack.

She took another deep breath and looked back at herself in the mirror.

"Do it," she said.

She spun around and walked straight to the laptop. Without another thought, she clicked on the buy button. She held her breath as the website processed her credit card. A moment later she saw a page that said, "Your ticket purchase has been confirmed. Have a great trip!"

Skylar almost couldn't believe it. She was going to Europe. By herself. The day after tomorrow.

She yelled out loud and started doing a happy dance.

CHAPTER FOURTEEN

"Hey! What do you think you're doing?" Bass yelled out the window of his car.

The day after meeting with Mary, he was at a gas station off the I-5 freeway, headed north. Even though they didn't speak of Kathy specifically, somehow Mary guilted Bass into going up to see his mom. Bass stopped off to fuel up for the road trip.

I sat quietly, and invisibly, in the backseat, watching everything. As Bass moved his car towards a gas pump, a lady cut in from the other side, got out, and loosened the gas cap on her car. Bass got out of his car and yelled again.

"Hey, excuse me! What do you think you're doing?"

"Sorry, what?" the lady asked. She stood by an older sedan with rust spots in the paint.

"You cut right in front of me. I was backing in to this pump."

A few people stared. A guy in a small delivery truck watched from his driver's seat. Another lady looked up from her phone.

"I, I didn't see you," the lady said as she put the gas pump in the car.

"Seriously lady! You know what you were doing. Super lame."

"I'm so sorry. I'm in a big hurry. I promise I didn't see you backing in."

Bass looked at her car, and in the backseat saw two girls looking out the window. They glanced back and forth between their mom and him.

"Look," he said. "Sorry for yelling. I'm in a hurry too. Maybe next time you'll be more aware of other people."

"OK," the lady said, nodding.

He caught the eye of the guy watching in his truck, who shook his head in annoyance, but Bass just shrugged his shoulders. He got back in his SUV and waited, keeping an eye on the lady in his rearview mirror. She looked like she was genuinely trying to hurry. She kept looking at Bass and then over to her girls. When she put the pump back, she gave Bass a quick wave and said, "Thank you." One kid waved from the back window.

Bass gave a head nod in the mirror and backed into the spot as she left. He got out and started to pump the gas.

"Be more aware of other people," said a voice that came from behind. "Good words to live by."

Bass turned to see a redheaded woman wearing an old-time golf outfit, complete with a pink sweater vest and plaid knickers. She wore a tweed cap that floated on her nest of red hair.

She stepped forward and said, "Hi Bassy!"

He stumbled backwards and bumped into his car, making Rebekah laugh.

"Yes, hilarious," he grumbled. He pulled his hands-free out of his pocket, not wanting to be seen talking to himself at a gas station.

"What are you doing here?" Bass said. "You know, I haven't even said yes to you guys, yet you still keep hounding me. Jacob practically killed me in the ocean and Mary scared me into thinking my life is gonna fail. I still think I'm going crazy. So, what are you here to do?"

"I'm doing my job, Bassy. I'm the love angel. I get to help you love everyone."

"Yeah, good luck with that." The pump clicked off and Bass topped up the gas, then replaced the nozzle. He turned to Rebekah, but she wasn't there. He looked around and saw that she was already sitting in the passenger's seat inside his SUV. Bass got in and saw Rebekah going through his music list.

"See anything you like?" he said.

"It could be better. But there's some promise here." Rebekah looked down at Bass's feet.

"Yep, thought so," she said.

"Thought what?"

"An old friend once told me that you can tell everything you need to know about a person by the music they listen to and the shoes they wear."

"I only wear flip-flops," Bass said. "And what's wrong with my music?"

"I didn't say anything was wrong. Just that it could be better." She continued scrolling through the playlist. "Ah yes, there's hope. You've got some 80s ballads in here. We can make this work."

"Make what work?"

"Why, to help you find your life's greatest treasure, of course!" Rebekah spoke in a tone that matched her old-time golf outfit.

Bass couldn't help but grin.

"There it is—a smile," she said. "This is going to be easier than I thought."

He put the car in drive and headed towards the freeway.

"Where are we headed?" Rebekah asked.

"In the last couple of days, I've been feeling guilty for not spending enough time with my mom when she came to visit. Plus, she asked for my help decorating her new place. I'm pretty good at that stuff so I'm going up there for two days."

"Just two?"

"Yeah, I'm super busy with work right now with some big goals I'm trying to hit."

Rebekah hit the 80s ballads playlist and turned up the volume.

"Wait, how did you do that? I thought you guys are just spirits or something?"

"Yes, we are, but we can also do whatever we want to here. Within reason, of course. Playing 80s music? Totally acceptable."

"But when I tried to touch Mary, I didn't feel anything."

"That's on you, Bassy. You need to be worthy. You can't just reach out and touch refined heavenly beings like us and expect to feel something, can you? You've got some work to do, amigo."

Bass got onto the freeway, veered into the left lane, and set the cruise control for 85mph, 15 over the speed limit. "What kind of work are you talking about?"

"All in good time. Besides, are you going to let us work with you or not?"

"I still don't even know if you're totally real."

"So Jacob's little show of force with the waves wasn't enough to convince you?"

Bass considered it. If he was being honest, it was. He'd never taken a spill like that when surfing. He also never rode a wave as big and long as the one he went in on. He knew Jacob made it happen. He saw him do it. Somehow, he controlled the ocean.

"So what if I say yes? What does that even mean?"

"Yes!" Rebekah made a fist pump with her hand like a 10-year-old boy. "If we get to work with you, I'm going to teach you how to love, which is really the most important thing in this life." She smiled and added, "Which makes me the most important angel in your council."

Bass laughed out loud.

"Can the others hear you?"

"Oh, they know." She made a quick glance towards the back seat where I sat. "Everyone wants to be the love angel."

A COUNCIL OF ANGELS

"But what do you mean? You'll teach me how to love? I've loved people." He thought immediately of Brittany. Then his mind raced to his recent dream, where he was with his parents and a new girl.

"I'm going to teach you to love God and to love others."

"Others?"

"Yes, like everyone." Rebekah looked at a billboard advertising an internet service. It featured a family all staring at screens and smiling. "Everyone, like everyone, is part of God's family. That means they're part of your family. The best way for you to love God, is to love the people here."

Bass wasn't convinced. He had a million questions about God. The whole thing never seemed logical to him. He opened his mouth to speak, but Rebekah looked directly at him and cut him off.

"I know what you're about to ask, Bassy, but let me just give you a quick example." She took off her tweed hat and placed it on the dashboard.

"What if," she started in a more somber tone, "I told you that the lady that cut in front of you at the gas station was on her way to the hospital? And what if I told you that she was in a hurry because the doctor called her to come in because he had some critical information about her youngest daughter? And what if I told you that her daughter's skin has been yellowish, especially around the eyes, and she hasn't eaten any food for four days?"

Bass immediately regretted yelling at her.

Rebekah continued. "What if I told you that woman lost her husband two years ago due to liver failure? And what if I told you that now she's scared to death it's happening all over again with her daughter?"

Bass glanced over at her long enough to see Rebekah was completely serious.

"Is that true?" he asked.

Rebekah sighed. "Yes, it's true. Right now, that woman is

arriving at the hospital. She's going to find out that yes indeed, her sweet little princess needs a liver transplant or else she's going to pass away within the week."

Bass's stomach knotted up with guilt, and he felt horrible for yelling at her. He tried to speak, but his throat tightened. He swallowed hard. "Is…is there anything I can do?"

"For her? Right now? No. But don't worry. There's another council already on it."

"You mean like other angels?"

"Yep," Rebekah said.

Although he didn't know how, Bass felt better. He let out a sigh and sank a little in his seat.

"This is just one tiny little lesson for you, Bassy. You need to be more aware of other people. You need to love them. And I'm going to show you how, if you let me that is." She paused and shot another glance in my direction. A mischievous look formed on her face. "And the rest of the council wants to help too, I suppose. Promise me you'll think about it?"

"Yes," Bass said. "I'll think about it."

"Outstanding!"

She put her finger on her cheek, made a screwing motion, and turned her face into a smile. She faded almost instantly, leaving the tweed hat on the dashboard.

CHAPTER FIFTEEN

Bass opened the window in the front room. He loved the smell of the salty air coming in from California's central coastline. He arrived the night before and after a lazy morning, he started helping his mom with her new place.

"I still think Monterey is for old people," Bass said. "But I gotta admit, I love this ocean breeze. It smells good here."

"Well, you get that in Huntington, don't you?" Kathy asked. "You live in the fancy numbered streets. You're closer to the beach than I am."

"Yeah, but I've got the traffic of PCH between me and the ocean. It's not the same. It feels cleaner here. Fresher."

Bass looked at his mom's new place. It was a small but nice mother-in-law unit and the couple that owned the main property was very nice, but traveled a lot. Kathy liked her home because it was in the heart of Monterey. It was also close to the hospital, where she worked as a respiratory therapist. When she wasn't at work, she was either golfing or researching her family history, and it showed.

Nothing else in the small house was set up yet, but her golf clubs were right by the door and her computer station had a prominent space in the front room. She had a three-monitor setup with a system that would make most programmers jealous. On the desk, next to the monitors, was a heap of notebooks, photo albums, books on the history of various cities, and more.

"OK, Mom, if we're gonna really get busy, I need some music. Can we stream something on your fancy computer?"

"Yes, what would you like to listen to?"

Bass thought for a moment and said, "How about some 80s music? You cool with that?"

"Anything that will bring out your creative genius," Kathy said, looking around the room. "Obviously, I'm not great at this stuff." She hit the play button and music filled the small home.

Bass clapped his hands together in a loud smack. "Let's get started with your paintings and pictures. Are these the boxes over here?"

"Yes," Kathy said. She moved towards the stack of boxes nestled in the corner. She lifted a small one from the top but suddenly fell backwards.

"Mom! Are you OK?"

She put her hand over her heart and was breathing deeply, in through her nose and out through her mouth.

"Yes, honey. I'm fine. Every now and then my heart does a little jumping jack. No big deal."

"Yes, it could be. Seriously Mom, are you OK?"

Kathy bent down to pick up the box. "Yes, you see?" she said, carrying the box. "Totally fine."

Bass opened his mouth again to say something, but she interrupted. "I'm in healthcare, Bass. It's nothing. But, can you get this box? It's too heavy for me." She smiled and used her foot to tap a large box with frames in it.

Bass pulled the box into the center of the room and ripped it open. He removed all the frames and rested them against the walls. A song came on that he didn't like. It reminded him of Brittany.

"Mom, can you skip to the next song?"

"No problem. Actually, why don't you come over here? I want to show you something."

Bass walked up to the desk. As he got closer, he saw how deeply invested she really was with her genealogy hobby. Her notebooks were full of scribbles and post-it notes.

"I just wanted to show you this one thing," she said.

Bass sighed. "No, mom. I told you before. I don't care about that stuff. So what if we have kings and queens in our past? I do not care."

"You should care, Bass. These people make up who you are. They each had a life and a story. Some of them did crazy things, like leaving their home countries and starting new lives." Kathy clicked open a file. He was impressed at how fast she was on her computer.

"Here, see? Check this guy out. He was one of your father's ancestors. He literally worked with Benito Juárez in Oaxaca, Mexico. It's your heritage, you know."

Bass sighed again. "Yeah, everyone seems to be telling me that lately. Besides, I don't even know who that guy is. And I gotta ask, did you get me up here just to show me this stuff? I'm glad it's a cool hobby for you, but it does nothing for me."

Kathy closed the files on her computer, lowered her head, and muttered. "I know, Bass. It's been my hope that you would want to learn more, but I get it. This isn't for everyone." She rested her forehead on her hand and said, "I do this to…" she paused, "Well, I do it to feel close to your father."

Bass took a step back. "Mom."

"I know, I know. You don't want to talk about him either. I understand that. And I respect that. I've hardly ever brought it up. It's something for you to work out. But for me, learning about him and his ancestry, your ancestry…it helps me remember him."

Bass wanted to object, but he paused. He wondered if

Rebekah was listening. If she was, how would she want him to speak to his mother?

"Maybe sometime in the future I'll be into this stuff. For now, I've got a business to grow. It's literally all I think about. Besides surfing, of course."

"OK, this might be a bad time, but I was thinking about asking you if you could go to a couple of libraries for me while you're in Spain."

"Mom!"

"OK, OK, I had to ask. You've got ancestors there. In reality, you've got ancestors from practically all over Europe. When you go there, you might be walking the same streets people from your past did."

Bass was running out of patience. "Let's just crank the 80s music and see if we can get this stuff hung on the walls, OK?"

Kathy looked at him. "Deal. But only if I can take you out for Mexican food for dinner?"

"You just don't stop with the ancestry thing, do you?"

"What? I thought you liked tacos."

They both laughed. Kathy stood and opened another box next to her computer. She sorted through some notebooks and said, "I know I'm persistent, but if there's one thing I've learned in life, it's when an opportunity presents itself, you've got to take it."

Her words sunk deep into Bass's mind. Kathy continued to speak, but he was no longer listening. He knew what he needed to do.

CHAPTER SIXTEEN

The day after getting home from the two-day visit with his mom, Bass went for a walk along the bike path which paralleled PCH. According to the council, it was my turn to chat with him. I followed him as he moved down the path, waiting for the right time.

It didn't take super mind-reading angel powers to tell he was lost in thought. He thought about his mom and felt sad that she might be lonely. He thought about his upcoming trip to Europe. He and JP were leaving in just two days. He wanted to be more excited, but had no idea what to expect. JP was going to look for girls, but Bass mostly cared about seeing something new.

He thought about Brittany when a guy moving fast on his bike yelled. "Get out of the bike lane, you moron!"

Bass started to flip him off, but decided against it. He wasn't sure if the angels were watching or not. Still, he had a pet peeve for cowards.

Sure, that guy can yell at me as he's speeding away, he thought.

Bass walked down the path towards the pier. It was late in the afternoon and the local artists and farmers were busy selling at the weekly street fair. He admired some paintings and liked how the artist used bold colors and thick brushstrokes.

"If you buy one today, you get 30% off the second painting," the artist said. He had long red hair with a scruffy, tobacco-stained face. He wore a giant wool sweater that looked like it was made in Peru.

"I'm just looking," Bass said. "But it's all good stuff."

"They make splendid gifts. Maybe something for a lady friend?"

"Currently don't have one..." Bass replied. He shrugged and walked towards the steps on the north side of the pier. He sat down and watched the people all around.

In front of him on the beach, a toddler cried because her older brother stomped on her sand castle. A gray-haired woman wearing pink pants and an overly thick coat shuffled down the path. A middle-aged guy walked past, talking loudly about closing some deal and seemed to want the entire world to listen in.

Next to him, a family waxed up their surfboards. A mother, father, teenage son, and three girls. The son threw a chunk of surf wax at one of the girls. She picked it up and threw it back at him even harder. The mom yelled something while the dad laughed to himself.

Bass looked past the family to the waves. They were blown-out and only a few surfers were trying to catch a lucky wave.

"It sure is beautiful, isn't it?"

Bass turned and saw me sitting next to him.

"How'd you get here? I mean, how do you guys just show up?"

"Honestly, I have no idea how it works. I'm still learning that myself."

Bass looked at me, sizing me up. I was wearing khakis and flip-flops with a white guayabera.

"Are you guys going to hassle me until I let you help me find my treasure or whatever?"

"No. Everyone already took their turn. I'm the final shot. If you say no, we'll leave you alone but, we really want this for you."

Bass looked back out towards the ocean. I knew what he was going to ask, but waited for him to make the move. Finally he said, "It's just hard for me to accept help, you know? I've done everything by myself. Besides, you guys are asking me to do something that I have no clue where to even start."

"What do you have to lose?"

Bass didn't answer immediately, and I pushed it a bit further. "You have a team of angels willing to help you find your life's greatest treasure. To me, that sounds pretty great."

Bass nodded, looked back at me, and asked, "Why the 40 days? It's so random. Why not 31 or 67?"

"No clue. But I *do* know we need some kind of deadline to push you. 40 days seems to work. Besides, it's kind of a religious number already, isn't it?"

"Yeah, that thing is still a little hard for me," Bass said. "It's just that I don't totally believe all of this, you know?"

"What do you mean?"

Bass looked out to the pier and the waves crashing into the pilings. "All of it. God, angels, religion. It doesn't make sense to me."

"Why is that?"

"Because, look at everything that's going on."

"All of what?"

"All of the struggle, disorder, hatred. There are so many bad things going on in this world." He ran his fingers through his hair. "Seriously, it just seems that God, if he exists, created a pretty imperfect world. There's so much wrong with this place. Like I said, it doesn't make sense to me. Never has."

I felt honored that Bass confided in me, so I felt I could dig a little deeper.

"What you're saying is true. This place isn't perfect and a lot of bad things happen."

"So God makes those things happen?"

"No, but he doesn't always stop them from happening either."

"Why not?"

"Well, what would that look like?"

"I don't know. Every time someone is about to do something wrong, he could just step in and stop it. No more abandoned babies. No more mass shootings. No more bombings. Stuff like that."

"To be clear, you would like God to step in every time anyone is about to make a wrong choice?"

"Yeah," Bass said, sounding less convinced.

"What kind of life would that be? We don't have to talk about the world. Let's talk about you. The next time you yell at someone who's smoking or beats you to a gas pump, you want God to step in and stop you?"

Bass thought for a moment. It hit close to home for him, just like I wanted it to. As a fiercely independent person, I could tell it bothered him, but I pushed further.

"It would be almost as if we were all children in a classroom and the teacher watched and dictated our every move. Is that what you're thinking?"

"I guess not." He fell silent for a moment. He ran his hand through his hair again and looked back at me. "So it's about freedom then?"

"Yeah, sometimes people call it personal agency or free will."

"It's like a double-edged sword then. We get to choose what we do but all of us will make bad choices."

"You will also make good choices," I added.

"Right. So what does God even do? Just sit back and watch the chaos?"

"He teaches us. He gives us the knowledge of right and wrong and then he hopes we make the right decision. But," I said

A COUNCIL OF ANGELS

holding up my finger, "he lets us make our own choices, even when they're wrong."

"OK, I get that he's not gonna interfere with every aspect of our lives or make our choices for us. I can accept that. And some people will make bad choices and those choices hurt others. It's logical, I suppose. Sucky, but logical. But what about the good stuff? Can't he help that along?"

"Why do you think I'm here?"

Bass smiled. I smiled back. I couldn't help it. I connected with the kid. He knew it. I knew it. I felt myself fading, even though I wanted to stay longer. I wanted to say more. I wanted to help more, but apparently I was out of time.

CHAPTER SEVENTEEN

The next day, Bass sat in his office at work, staring at a spread-sheet. He hadn't typed a single thing in over 20 minutes. I sat in an empty chair in the corner, recording everything.

There was a quick knock and Bass turned to see Mr. Tight Pants Man opening the door. He poked his head in and said, "Hey Bass, we're going to have a quick powwow in about an hour. I sent you an invite but can tell you haven't seen it."

"What's it about?"

"We'll discuss it at the meeting."

"I'm not going unless it relates to my company," Bass said.

Derrick closed his eyes and made an exaggerated sigh, his belly sinking further over his belt. "Yes, of course it's about your company. Jen wants you there. Just be there."

"All right."

Just as Derrick walked away, the room changed as the other angels began to appear.

Mary was first. "Hello Sebastian."

He jumped in his chair. "Oh, hey," he said. "Yeah, actually, this isn't a good time. I've got a lot to do."

"Have you been doing it?"

84

A COUNCIL OF ANGELS

"Umm..." Bass trailed off.

"Hey, slugger," Jacob said from behind Bass. He wore silver pants and a silver vest with a white shirt. Next to Jacob, Rebekah appeared wearing a French mime outfit complete with suspenders and face paint.

She walked up to Bass and pretended to speak, but made no sound. She did the whole caught-behind-glass routine but wasn't very good at it.

"Oh brother," Jacob said. "Gimme a break."

"You know you like it," she said.

"Ha! I knew you couldn't keep up with the mime bit," Jacob gloated. He turned to Bass and spoke out of the side of his mouth. "She likes to talk too much."

Rebekah punched him on the shoulder.

Mary nodded to me, and I suddenly felt myself becoming visible.

"Hi Bass," I said.

He gave me a quick nod and then reached for his cell phone and paced around the office like he was on a call.

"Guys, seriously, I can't do this right now. I'm leaving for Europe like tomorrow, and I have no clue what this meeting is about."

"We'll be fast, Bassy," Rebekah said.

"Super fast," Jacob said. "You in or you out? Easy as that."

"You mean, doing whatever it is you guys want me to do? Yeah, I don't know."

I stepped forward. I couldn't help myself. "Bass, what do you have to lose?"

"Umm...I mean, I have no clue what you guys want me to do, and it's really bad timing. I feel so close to getting my company to where I finally want it."

Mary said, "That's the point, Bass. We're not asking you to give up anything. We're simply inviting you to do more. More that will help you."

85

"Look tiger, we already said it as clear as we can get. We're here to help you find your life's greatest treasure. Let that sink in. What do you seriously have to lose?"

Rebekah opened her mouth like she was going to say something, but closed it and nodded to me.

"It's got to be your choice," I said. "But we will do all we can to help you."

Bass stopped pacing and stared at me, thinking. "What if I say yes? Am I going to be some sort of do-gooder going around tossing out rainbows and furry little kittens?"

"That sounds fun!" Rebekah said laughing.

"No, Sebastian," Mary said. "We're going to help you right your world."

"What? No. I can't fight all the world's problems."

"You're absolutely right. You can't and you shouldn't."

Bass looked confused.

"Wait, what?"

"We don't want you to fight anything, Bass. We want you to solve things," Mary said.

He started to roll his eyes, but caught himself. "OK, I get it. So I should try to *solve* the world's problems?"

"You can't. Not by yourself," Jacob said. "But you can start right here, right now. You'd be amazed what changes you can make when a council of angels has your back. Besides, Mary should have emphasized *your* in the sentence. Like, 'we're going to help you right *your* world'. Make sense?"

"Yeah, I guess."

"Come on, Bassy. We all know you already made up your mind at your mom's house," Rebekah said. "You're just playing hard to get."

Bass looked down, trying to hide his guilty smile. He looked up at me and I stared straight back, nodding my head. He looked at Mary, searching for approval.

"OK. Let's do this. How does this work? Do I call out your names or something? Are you always going to be stalking me?"

Jacob shot a glance over to me but quickly said, "We're going to give you a whistle."

"A whistle?"

"Yeah, it's shaped like a bird and you just give it a little tweet anytime you need us," Jacob said.

Bass looked down to the ground, obviously confused, so he didn't see Jacob give Rebekah a wink. Rebekah covered her mouth to keep from laughing.

Personally, I didn't know the answer to Bass's question. Mary, smiling at Jacob's joke, explained, "No, Sebastian, we are *not* going to give you a whistle. When you need us, we'll know."

"I assume you can come to Europe with me? Did I mention I'm leaving tomorrow?"

"Yes!" Rebekah shouted. "I love Europe this time of the year. Especially Paris, as you can tell," she said, pointing to her outfit. "It turns out I get to teach you to love, literally in one of the most romantic cities in the world. I'm so excited."

"What? How do you know that?"

"Au revoir," Rebekah said, blowing a kiss at Bass as she faded away.

Jacob and Mary disappeared immediately after. Bass turned and looked at me and I felt myself fading too, but I managed a quick wave. He waved back.

CHAPTER EIGHTEEN

"I think sporks are the perfect utensil," JP said. He examined the spork in his hand, the way a chemist handles a test tube.

"I think sporks only ever accompany really bad, prepackaged meals," Bass replied, using his spork to pick through the inflight meal. He sifted through what the package said were potatoes to try and find what the package said was chicken.

"When we get back, I'm gonna throw away all of my forks and spoons and buy a bunch of sporks instead," JP said.

"You do that, buddy."

JP picked up his spork, rubbed it clean with his shirt, looked at it again approvingly, and then put it carefully into his backpack.

He then looked back at Bass and examined him for a minute. "I'm gonna pretend that you're having the time of your life. You're a rich, single dude on his way to the motherland with his best friend. Your life is about as perfect as it can be. The one thing that's missing, a beautiful woman, is waiting for you in Europe."

"Yes," Bass said, "you've mentioned that before."

"I speak the truth. You'll see." JP changed his tone, becoming more serious but also more sympathetic. "Seriously though, what's the deal? You haven't said much."

Bass ran a hand through his hair and let out a long sigh. He wadded up his napkin and threw it on top of the prepacked airplane meal. It didn't taste good, anyway.

"Jen's going to sell her company," he said.

"What does that mean?"

"I don't know, but it sucks. I just found out yesterday. I don't know what it means to my own company. She owns 30% of it and I rely on her manufacturing and employees to make my stuff. The new buyer might come in and change everything. She didn't exactly share the details with me."

"Did you ask her about that? She knows you want to sell your company too, right?"

"Yes, and she's onboard with that, but her loyalty is to her own business first. I'm pretty sure she wants to retire."

"Did she steal that idea from you?"

"Probably." Bass took the plastic cup and shook the ice cubes around. He looked out the rectangle window to a dark sky. They were 35,000 feet somewhere over the Atlantic ocean. It made him feel small. Maybe his life wasn't as perfect as he thought it was. In one 30 minute meeting, his entire future was now unclear.

"So what am I supposed to do now? I'm literally flying away from the one place where I can do anything and we'll be gone for two weeks."

"Europe has Wi-Fi you know."

"Yeah. I'll just have to make it work."

"Dude, once you see Italian chicks, you won't even remember your little t-shirt business. I promise."

Just then, a pale-skinned young woman with black hair and hazel eyes turned around from the seat in front of JP. With a heavy French accent, she said, "Do not waste your time with Italian girls. They are not worth the fight. And don't even try to speak to a French woman, at least, not while wearing that ridiculous baseball hat."

JP removed his red ball cap and held it in his hands as if he were handling a brand new baby kitten. "My hat?" he asked, his voice dropping to a defeated tone. "But I like this hat."

"It's your choice, mon amie. A European girl or your darling hat." She gave him a Mona Lisa smile and turned back around.

JP put a cupped hand to his mouth and whispered, "Has she been listening to us the entire time?"

Bass shrugged.

"Did I say anything stupid?"

"You always say something stupid," Bass whispered back.

JP shook his fist at Bass. "One of these days, buddy. One of these days."

Bass grinned while JP put his ball cap into his backpack next to his new spork.

"How does my hair look?"

"American. Very American."

JP shook his head, adjusted his floral-print neck pillow, closed his eyes, and started snoring in almost record time. Bass returned to looking out the plane window, thinking about his future.

PART II

TO SEE

April 20, 6:00 a.m.

Greetings Team,

Bass accepted the challenge! Thank you so much for doing your part to help him.

As you know, now is when the fun begins (although Bass probably won't see it that way). You can understand why the next little while might be hard for me to watch.

As always, I'll do my best to stay out of the way and simply record what I see. It's already been so illuminating having access to Bass's thoughts and daily life.

Warm Regards,
   Michael

CHAPTER NINETEEN

"They call it 'the tube,'" JP said, smiling like an idiot. "I freaking love this, dude!"

"How are you not tired?" Bass asked in disbelief at JP's energy, feeling his own desire to sleep where he stood.

After flying through the night, they arrived in London early the following morning. They tried to reset their biological clocks by staying awake through the day. Bass was struggling, but JP didn't seem to be phased as they raced along London's underground train system.

They raced along the Jubilee line towards St. John's Wood Station, the closest stop to the famous Abbey Road. JP loved The Beatles ever since his mother introduced their music to him when he was a kid. It was his lifelong dream to walk across Abbey Road, just like John, Paul, George, and Ringo did for their album cover. He was literally named after both John and Paul. Now that they were getting close, he could hardly contain himself.

It was late afternoon, and the tube was jam-packed with people commuting back home. Bass wasn't thrilled about being close to so many people. He was used to his own space—his own car, his own house, and sometimes even his own beach.

Ever since they got on the tube, it seemed like more people got on than got off. Bass wondered if there would be room for any more bodies. He and JP stood and shared a steel pole in the middle of the train.

Bass noticed a gray-haired woman working her way through the train towards them. She silently handed out papers. She got closer to him and offered him a small card. She looked into his eyes for just a moment before moving on and gave a faint smile.

Bass looked at the card in his hand. It read:

I am deaf. Any donations are very welcome.

Bass flipped the card and saw a quote which said:

Could a greater miracle take place than for us to look through each other's eyes for an instant?
-Henry David Thoreau

Bass turned and noticed the woman coming back towards him. Most people returned the cards to her. One person handed her some change. When she got to Bass, he pulled out 50 pound note from his wallet and gave it to her. Her eyes got big, and she signed, "thank you" and smiled at him.

He put his wallet back in his pocket. He tried to hand her the card, but she caught his hand, gently pushing it against his chest, clearly wanting him to keep it. She looked deeply into his eyes and then moved past him. He put the card in his other pocket.

Bass looked at JP, who was beaming. "Admit it, you love this place."

"Yes," Bass said, "I have to admit, London is pretty cool—in the three hours I've been awake to enjoy it, that is."

"And we're just beginning. Wait until we see Venice!"

The train slowed, and the crowd moved towards the doors.

"This is our stop, mate," JP said in a horrible British accent. They moved with the swarm of commuters through the station. When they reached the top of the stairs, a blast of freezing wind shot down into the corridor.

"Holy smokes! Why is it so cold?" Bass rubbed his hands together. "I thought it was supposed to be nice this time of the year."

"It's England, dude. It's not exactly Orange County."

Bass shoved his hands into his pockets to get warm, and his heart skipped a beat. His wallet wasn't there. "Dude! My wallet's gone." He dug in every pocket he had. Nothing.

"Serious?" JP said.

"Yeah, I just had it! You saw." He frantically searched the ground and ran back downstairs towards the train. He and JP dashed into the tunnel. Still nothing. They caught the attention of a security officer.

"Can I help you?"

"Yeah, my wallet's missing," Bass said. "I just had it when we were on this train. Now I can't find it."

"Are you certain, sir?"

"Yes, I'm sure," Bass replied, now agitated. "I'm screwed. All my cards were in there." Bass looked at the officer, but knew there was nothing he could do. The wallet was gone.

Bass gave him the name of their hotel and room number. "If by some miracle it shows up, can you please notify me?"

"Yes sir. I'm sorry to say theft is not uncommon. Bloody immigrants."

With that, Bass and JP headed out of the tube and towards Abbey road.

"Well, this is just perfect," Bass said. "Now I have no way to buy anything." He kicked a tree by the sidewalk. "Now what am I supposed to do? I'm in another country with no access to my money! I shouldn't have come on this trip."

"Dude, I've got plenty of dinero. I've got you. We'll call your banks and tell them what's up," JP said. "This kind of thing happens all the time."

Bass clenched his fists and paced back and forth, his mind racing. This kind of thing never happened to him. He worked his entire life to be independent and in less than five minutes, he felt like he'd lost everything. He was in another country and now he had to rely on someone else to provide for him.

JP tried to make forward progress. "Do you still have your passport?"

"Yeah, I left that at the hotel."

"Easy! Then all you need is some cash. I'm not rich like you but I'm doing all right."

Bass put his hands on his waist and continued pacing. He realized there was nothing he could do. After a minute, he glanced back at JP, who looked between a map on his phone and the street signs nearby. They were only a few blocks from Abbey road. Bass inhaled deeply through his nose, then breathed out slowly, venting his frustration. "OK. I'm sorry, man. And thank you for being willing to help."

JP looked up from his phone, put a hand over his heart, and looked upward. "It's what I do."

Bass looked up and noticed the sun coming out from behind the clouds. Then he saw a red double-decker bus moving up the street. He'd only seen those in the movies, and now he was living it.

JP meandered in the direction of Abbey road. "Shall we?"

"Yeah, let's go walk on a famous street," Bass said. He looked at JP, who had switched from meandering to bouncing. "Doesn't anything get you down?"

"Not when we're this close to fulfilling one of my childhood dreams!" He started walking faster. "Besides, it wasn't my wallet."

CHAPTER TWENTY

"I'm serious. They taste totally different here. Just try some."

JP handed Bass a handful of M&M's. They sat on the waterfront with the Tower Bridge behind them. With a good night's sleep, Bass felt refreshed and was enjoying the day. Thinking about it, he had to admit he was astounded by what he saw in London.

He took a few of JP's M&M's and popped them into his mouth. JP nodded, his eyebrows raised. "See? I told you, dude."

"Yeah, sure, I don't know. I hardly eat these things."

"They have a distinct flavor," JP said, staring at the bridge as he thought intently. "I've got it! It's malt. They have a malt flavor. They're like Whoppers." He laughed out loud. "Nailed it."

"I can't believe we flew across our entire country and over the Atlantic ocean just to go to a store that we have at home."

"They don't taste like this at home, man. These are better."

"Well, you know what I want to buy?"

"What?"

"Some freaking pants! This place is freezing."

"You're the smart guy that came to Europe with only shorts."

"How was I supposed to know? It's springtime. I mean, it's actually sunny. Shouldn't it be warm, too?"

JP let out a laugh and put an entire handful of M&M's into his mouth. Then, without even chewing, he said, "Let's…" he stopped talking as he sucked in some saliva, "let's go back over to that Piccadilly Circus area again. There were a ton of stores there where you can probably get some pants. Maybe even get a little British lassie to help you out."

"Lassie? That's Scottish. Besides, are you still on that? We haven't seen a single attractive woman here."

"Are you crazy? They're all over!" JP spewed chocolate pieces out of his mouth. "Plus, that accent—come on, you gotta love the accent."

"Yeah, the accent is cool. Let's go."

Bass and JP made their way to one of the bus stops. They looked down the street and watched a red double-decker making its way towards them.

"How much you wanna bet it stops right here?" JP said, pointing to the road just to the left of him.

"Nah, it's gonna stop here." Bass pointed directly in front of him. The bus got closer and slowed.

"Wait for it. Wait for it," JP said. The bus hugged the curb and JP stepped back. It stopped directly in front of Bass, who smiled smugly at JP.

"I win."

Just then, a lady carrying a bunch of small boxes cut in front of him as the doors opened. Behind her, a group of teenagers pushed their way forward onto the bus.

"Um, dude? Check it out," JP said, pointing up to the bus windows.

The bus was jammed full of people.

"Yeah, I'm not getting on that," Bass said.

"I didn't think you would. Take our chances with the tube?"

"Sure."

A COUNCIL OF ANGELS

"Hey, look at the bright side, at least you won't get your wallet stolen."

"You're hilarious."

They made their way through the London Underground system. Bass watched everyone suspiciously. It surprised him at how many people were reading. But then again, he'd never really commuted in his life. He'd certainly never ridden on a train to go back and forth to work. He wondered if any of these people had seen or spoken to an angel and then it occurred to him, for helping him find his life's treasure, they sure weren't hanging around very much.

When Bass and JP arrived at Piccadilly Circus Station, they got off the train and walked to the stairs leading out. Upon hitting the open air, they were shocked at how busy the street was.

They ambled through the crowd towards the Shaftesbury Memorial Fountain. There was some commotion, and Bass saw a couple of teenagers running through the crowd and yelling. They came in fast and one of the guys knocked a few people out of the way, causing a chain reaction. Right in front of him, a middle-aged woman with a leopard print hat fell backwards. Bass bent down immediately to help.

"Are you OK?" he asked, holding his hand out to her.

The woman took a second to compose herself and then took his hand. "Yes, yes," she said. "Thank you, love."

Bass steadied her by the arm as she stood. She straightened her clothing, smiled at him, and continued on. He felt someone staring at him and looked up at the fountain. Sitting there was a girl in her 20s with strawberry blond hair. She had a backpack at her feet with a book in her hands. She wasn't reading though— she was staring directly at him.

As he looked at her face, a tingling sensation ran down his spine. She was familiar somehow. He maintained eye contact as long as he could, but she didn't look away, and it quickly became

101

a challenge. The traffic light changed, and he got caught in the crowd as everyone moved. He quickly glanced at JP, who was already crossing the street. He looked back to the girl, who was still staring at him.

Bass almost hit a streetlight but swerved at the last minute. He finally caught up to JP.

"What was that all about?"

"What?" Bass replied, playing dumb.

"You know what. I saw the whole thing, tough guy."

Bass shook his head. "I don't know what you're talking about."

"And you think there aren't any pretty girls in England."

CHAPTER TWENTY-ONE

After two solid days in London, Bass and JP hopped on a flight to Berlin. It was an early morning flight and JP was already asleep on his floral-print neck pillow. He let out a heavy snore and people across the aisle looked over. Bass elbowed him and he jerked awake.

"Sup?" JP said in a voice too loud for the quiet airplane. He looked around cluelessly, and then closed his eyes again.

Bass rummaged through his backpack for his headphones to try and squeeze in some podcasts before landing on German soil. He checked his phone to see a notification from his bank. They put a hold on his cards and luckily, there was no activity. Whoever had his wallet wasn't using his money.

An hour later, Bass and JP landed in Berlin. They rented a car at the airport and set out to explore the city. JP drove while Bass tried to navigate. They headed towards a sign that said, "Tiergarten." They took a road that drove right past a beautiful park.

Ahead of them, on the right-hand side of the road, they noticed a guy trying to push a car. Instantly, the mother from the gas station with the ill daughter flashed into Bass's mind.

"Dude, pull over!"

As soon as JP stopped, Bass got out and ran up to the guy, motioning to the car.

"Can I help you?"

The man smiled and nodded his head. Bass noticed a woman in the driver's seat with a young boy in the backseat.

He realized they were trying to push-start the car. He leaned in, pushed hard, and the car began to roll. JP caught up and pressed his shoulder against the bumper. It moved even faster. With a loud pop and a squeal of the tires, the car finally started. The woman revved the engine and put it into neutral.

"Danke," the man said and shook Bass's hand.

"Danke," Bass said back. "I mean, you're welcome."

The man nodded and shook JP's hand, too. Then he got into the car and the family slowly drove away. JP waved to the kid in the backseat, who waved back.

JP and Bass turned to go back to their car when Bass jammed his toe against the curb. As usual, he was only wearing flip-flops, so his toe took the full impact. He looked down and saw that the toenail on his right foot was broken in half, with blood already pouring out. The pain was exquisite. It began to throb as Bass screamed out.

"Dude, what happened?" JP asked.

Bass couldn't talk, as a salty flavor filled his mouth. He hobbled onto the grass, plopped down, and rocked back and forth. He pushed at the top of his foot, trying to relieve the pain. He punched the ground and fought hard not to cry.

"Do we have any napkins or anything?" he yelled.

JP came over and looked at Bass's toe.

"Oh, nasty!" he shouted. "I can't handle toe stuff. No way." He turned and walked towards the car, shaking his arms to rid himself of the chills. "I'll check, though," he shouted back. "I think I have something left over from lunch."

A minute later, Bass tenderly soaked up blood with a napkin. His toenail was bent in half, with the top part facing up. There was only one thing to do. He took a deep breath, gripped the loose piece of toenail, and ripped it off. He cried out loud and fell backwards, clenching his eyes shut and rolling on the grass.

"What'd you do?" JP yelled over. "No wait. Don't tell me." He had his hands on his knees, like he was about to dry heave.

Bass got up and tried his best to walk off the pain. He left the napkin on there as a sort of field bandage. Besides, the blood was already gluing it to his toe. He hobbled over to a bench, glanced down, and noticed a quote scratched into the wood.

Only a life lived for others is a life worthwhile
-Albert Einstein

"Yeah, right," Bass said out loud. He looked over at JP, who was watching him.

"You about done crying?" he asked.

"You about done dry heaving?" Bass shot back.

"Funny. I'll be in the car whenever you're ready to go. There's still a lot to see in this city."

Bass looked down at his toe again. It throbbed with every heartbeat.

"Tough break, sport," Jacob said. The large angel sat on the bench next to Bass. He wore an all-white lederhosen. He even had an alpine hat, complete with a silver feather in it.

"What the heck are you wearing?"

"Rebekah put me up to it. I like it. It hugs me just right."

Bass stared in disbelief. "Where have you guys been? I said yes to the little treasure thing, and then you disappeared on me. And by the way, I could have used an angel's help a couple of times already. Not sure if you know this or not, but I got robbed. And if you'll just look here," he said pointing at his foot, "I broke half my toenail off."

Jacob rubbed his chin and said, "Hmm...yeah, it looks pretty serious."

SEAN MARSHALL

Bass was sure the angel was being sarcastic. "Oh, and you wanna know how I did this?"

Jacob tilted his chin upward. "Enlighten me."

"I helped a family get their car going! If this is how God or the universe or whatever rewards helping people, I'm out. It's not for me."

"Let me see that foot," Jacob said. "Lift it up."

"What? No. It's gross. I can barely look at it."

"Trust me."

Bass lifted his leg towards the big angel. The throbbing intensified. Jacob closed his eyes and waved his hand over the foot, and the pain instantly subsided. Bass looked down to see the blood was gone, too.

"How'd you…?"

Jacob sat back on the bench, folded his arms, and grinned.

Bass picked the napkin off his toe. It was healed. The nail was still half gone, but it didn't hurt.

"Sorry, chief. The nail has to grow back on its own."

Bass couldn't believe it. He got up and walked around. His foot felt totally normal. "Thank you," he said.

"Did it feel good to help?"

"Yes, of course. I mean, I didn't get to enjoy that do-gooder feeling for very long though."

"Would you like to know something crazy?"

"Yeah."

"By helping that family, you got closer to who you really need to be more than anything you've ever done in your business."

"What? I practically broke my toe! I'm just supposed to sacrifice myself for the good of others?"

"You think about that for a minute," Jacob said. "Nobody has ever done anything for you?"

He knew where Jacob was going. He instantly thought of Kathy and how hard she worked, sometimes even two jobs, while

106

he was a kid. She put herself through school but still always managed to be there for the important things.

"Yeah, but that's not what I mean," Bass said. "I thought helping people would give me some kind of good karma."

"You mean what goes around comes around?"

"Yeah."

"Oh, it does. It's not always the way you think, but trust me, you get hooked up. And it's usually in greater proportion to what you gave."

Bass looked over to JP who was pouring over a map while sitting on the hood of the car.

"I better get going," Bass said. "Thank you for fixing my foot."

"Thank you for helping those people," Jacob said.

"Huh? How does that help you?"

"It's all connected. This whole thing depends on people making good choices."

Jacob stood up on the bench, cupped his hands in front of his mouth, and started yodeling.

Bass glanced around to see if anyone, like JP, could see or hear what was happening. JP was still studying the map. Bass looked back right as Jacob yodeled even louder and then disappeared.

CHAPTER TWENTY-TWO

After only one day in Berlin, Bass and JP hopped on an early morning flight to Paris. After checking in to their hotel, they left to explore the French capital. After an hour, they stood in the middle of the plaza in front of the Notre-Dame Cathedral. Their eyes followed the architecture all the way to the roof.

"I don't get it," JP said, "if this is a church, then why do they have those freaky-looking gargoyle things on it? It doesn't seem very, you know, holy. It's just scary."

"People say they're supposed to ward off the evil spirits," Bass said.

"But it's a church," JP shot back. "Shouldn't that be enough to drive the bad guys away? Do you think evil spirits are really fighting to get inside the church? I wouldn't. It's the last place I'd go if I were a bad guy."

Bass laughed and focused on the gargoyles. Blackened by weather over the centuries, they appeared to glare down at the visitors below. Still, the building was amazing. It made Bass think about why people would put so much effort into something.

He thought of his own business. He wasn't building something to last. He was building something to sell. Was that the

108

right thing to do? He thought about what his legacy might be. If it wasn't a company, then what?

The smell of cigarette smoke filled Bass's nose, and he turned and saw three guys roughly his own age walking past, all smoking.

"Don't these guys get it? Smoking isn't cool. They're literally paying money to give themselves cancer."

"Dude, you're in Europe. Everyone smokes here. It's all part of the experience." JP said. "Speaking of experience, let's find some crepes. We're in the motherland of crepes you know."

"Sounds good."

"Check it out," JP said pointing, "There's a crepe shop right across the street. I'll go get a couple and bring them back here. Ham and cheese or Nutella?"

"Ham and cheese, for sure. Thanks, man."

JP turned and jogged off through the plaza.

Bass sat down on a bench and continued to look at the cathedral.

A woman next to him spoke. "It is an interesting building, isn't it?"

Bass turned and saw Mary, who was wearing her usual white, flowing clothes. Her long, dark hair moved with the breeze. In the afternoon light, Bass thought she looked like someone he knew. Yet she looked so out of place in the old, gritty plaza.

"Are you sure people can't see you?" Bass asked.

Mary smiled.

"So, am I getting any closer to finding my life's greatest treasure?"

"What do you think?"

"No clue. Should I be searching for secret clues or something?"

Mary let out a short chuckle, nodded her head, and said, "Yes, I suppose you could say that."

"What do you mean? Where? How?"

He followed Mary's gaze as she stared across the plaza. JP was walking back with two crepes. He smiled, excited to eat them. A pigeon suddenly dived at him, but he ducked as it flew past. He dodged another one also, but he didn't see a crack in the pavement and tripped, falling face forward. The crepes flew out of his hands, landing on the concrete in front of him. Within seconds, pigeons swarmed around, feasting on a free lunch. JP got up, wadded the napkins, and threw them on the ground.

Bass felt bad, but couldn't help from laughing out loud. Mary smiled, but then said, "Watch."

JP looked up to Bass, shrugged his shoulders, and laughed. He turned to walk back to the crepe shop.

"It's amazing how nothing gets to that guy," Bass said.

"Yes, he's a special person."

"Did he already meet with his own council of angels?"

"No. He hasn't. The time may come when he will. It will depend on his choices."

Bass shooed away some pigeons walking near him. One, undeterred, continued towards him. Bass stood and kicked at the bird. It flew away, leaving two feathers floating down to the pavement.

"It's just a pigeon," Mary said.

"Yeah, nasty, rotten things full of diseases."

Mary looked back towards JP. "Sebastian, take a good look at JP. What's he doing right now? Really think about it."

Bass glanced over at his friend again. "Umm...buying crepes for us?"

"That's the specific act. How is he spending his time right now?"

"Being nice?"

"That's his emotional driver. But what's he actually doing? What's the overall general verb?"

Bass looked across the plaza to where JP was standing in line.

JP smiled and waved at a couple of girls walking past. Then it dawned on him.

"He's serving."

"Exactly," Mary said. "He volunteered to get the food for you two. He didn't even think twice about doing it. He just did it. Rebekah is right when she says that loving others is one of the most important lessons you could learn in this life. Love them by serving them."

"I feel like I've tried that a little bit already," Bass said.

"That's good. Now do more."

Bass cocked his head backwards and raised his eyebrows. "Yeah, I would probably get hurt somehow. I'd lose my wallet again or something else would happen."

"You're just out of practice. Do more."

Mary looked at Bass, who was pacing around the bench, keeping his eyes on the pigeons. "Sebastian, sit down for a moment. I promise the birds won't bother you."

She waved a hand and all the pigeons in the plaza suddenly flew away at once.

Bass plopped down next to Mary. "This is a big clue for you. Are you ready?"

Bass sat up and listened.

"Most people spend their entire life searching for happiness but never find it. You know why? They're looking for it in the wrong places."

Mary looked out at the people walking around in the plaza and continued. "Most people forget to serve others. They think of only themselves. On the other hand, think of all the greatest figures in human history. Often the most revered, are those who spent their lives in the service of others."

Bass looked up and noticed JP paying for the crepes.

"Sebastian, happiness comes to those who serve."

"Yeah, Jacob told me that before he almost killed me on a

wave." He thought about it for a second. That seemed so long ago.

"Yes, he always steals my best lines. I don't mind. It's true."

JP made his way back but walked cautiously, watching for any pigeons.

Mary stood up and said, "Sebastian, here's a little secret for you—the secret to happiness in your own life is found in serving others. Meditate on that for a while."

She faded right as JP showed up.

"Dude, did you see that? I made a fool of myself in front of all these fancy French people!"

"I know. It was awesome."

"Too bad you didn't get it on video. 'Dumb American makes fool of himself at Parisian landmark'. It could have gone viral!"

As JP handed Bass his crepe, he thought about happiness. He used to think he was happy, but now he wasn't sure.

JP sat down and already had a mouthful of crepe, blowing in and out quickly. "Ooh, ah. Hot!"

Bass smiled. "Thank you, man."

CHAPTER TWENTY-THREE

Later that evening, when they got back to their hotel, Bass checked his email. There was a message from Jen. It read:

Hey Bass-

Hope you're having a blast. Europe is really pretty this time of the year. Real fast, I have a buyer for my business. I'm moving forward.

We'll sort out the details of what it means to you when you get home. You're actually going to like it. There's just one minor detail I hope you'll be OK with. I think you will be.

Safe travels!
-Jen

Bass wondered what Jen's message meant. Then he saw an official-looking email from the Huntington Beach Police Station. It read:

Hello Mr. Martinez,

I hope you're well. I wanted to follow up with you about your accident. In doing a little more research for my report, I found the attached picture that I thought you might find interesting.

It's a photo taken from a traffic camera near your accident. It appears that just before the exact time of impact, a bright light was captured directly in front of the truck of Dan Johnson (the man who hit you). We haven't been able to identify what it was, but I believe it's what caused Mr. Johnson to swerve the way he did. Because he swerved, he hit you indirectly, which drastically lessened the damage.

We're determining if it was possibly a reflection from street lighting or if it was simply the headlights from another car. I've also looked at all the photos the camera took both before and after the accident. This is the only one where the light appears.

Either way, it's impressive to see. Take a look. I'll be in touch with any further details I find.

Best Regards,
Officer Curtis Gilbert

Bass clicked on the attached photo. It was grainy and exactly the way you'd expect a traffic camera photo to look. But Bass could clearly see the truck which hit him. He could also see the front tire of his motorcycle entering the frame.

In between the truck and his motorcycle, there was a bright light. At first, he thought it was just a glare, but as he looked closer, he noticed it had a form.

"It couldn't be," he said out loud.

CHAPTER TWENTY-FOUR

Bass woke up early. He looked around the fancy hotel room and out the window. They were in the heart of Paris. In the other bed, JP was still snoring away.

Bass showered quickly and got ready for the day. Feeling hungry, he nudged JP.

"Hey, I'm gonna get a bite to eat or something. I gotta get out of here."

JP grunted.

"Is it cool if I grab like 50 euros from your wallet?"

"Yeah, that's fine," JP mumbled. He turned and inhaled sharply with a slurping sound and wiped a patch of drool from his mouth.

"I'll be back in an hour or so."

Bass left the room and took the stairs down to the plaza below. After walking outside, he passed through a narrow alley to the main street where he'd seen some cafes. He shook his head with amazement—impressed with the sheer detail put into each building he saw. Bass thought the Parisians deserved every ounce of credit given for their beautiful city.

He finally made it out to the plaza and sat at the first open table. He took the menu from behind the napkin holder and glanced over it. Smoke wafted into his nose, and he turned to see an older woman with a cup of coffee and a cigarette. He shook his head in disgust, but she didn't notice.

A server came over and asked for his order. Bass tried his hand at French and said what sounded like, "Oon crosaunt cee vu play." He pointed to the menu, which showed a croissant with ham and cheese.

The server nodded and walked away.

Bass took out his phone, opened his messages, and decided to text Brittany. They'd spoken only in brief spurts since their breakup, but always via texts. He thought about it for a second and then started typing.

"Guess what?"

He left it intentionally short on purpose because he wanted her to engage. He stared at the screen for a second and then hit send.

He looked up to take in his surroundings. The plaza itself was incredible. Cafes lined the buildings, with small shops in between. Two pigeons moving towards him caught his attention. One was missing a foot with only a stump in its place. It limped as it walked, but kept up with the pigeon in front.

Bass looked at his phone, waiting for a response. Brittany always had her phone with her. The question was whether or not she would reply. Then he remembered he was half a day ahead of her. *It didn't matter*, he thought. *She's a night owl, anyway.*

He put his phone down as the server brought over his food. It was the fanciest croissant he'd ever seen. It was served on china, complete with a white linen napkin, knife, and fork.

Bass's phone lit up and the words "typing" appeared. She was responding. He sat up in his chair, grabbed his phone, and waited.

"What's up," came the text.

A COUNCIL OF ANGELS

Bass typed quickly. "Hey! I was thinking about you and figured I'd say hi. Guess where I'm texting you from?"

"Don't want to guess. Where?"

"Paris! As in Europe!"

After hitting the send button, Bass took a bite of the croissant. It was a perfect temperature, and the cheese was warm and melting. The buttery flavor erupted in his mouth.

Brittany texted back. "That's cool."

"I got in a wreck on my bike not too long ago. I'm good. Just some crazy road rash on one of my legs. JP talked me into coming to Europe because YOLO or whatever."

"You got in a wreck?"

"Yeah but no big deal."

Bass loved that she asked back. Maybe she cared, even a little.

"How's the business?"

"It's going well. Jen has some news for me, but I'm waiting until I get back. Actually trying to enjoy this vacation."

Bass saw the words "typing" start immediately after he sent his last text.

"It's your business. You should know exactly what's happening at all times."

"Right. Cool. Noted." Bass grimaced at her feistiness. He continued, "I can't remember if you've been to Paris before."

"Nope."

"Is everything cool? I mean, how have you been?"

"I'm good. What do you want?"

Bass was taken back by her directness.

"IDK, I just thought I'd say hi. Sorry I guess."

He regretted reaching out to her. He hated how weak he felt around her and how she always seemed to have the upper hand. He waited for another message, but she wasn't replying. He kept typing.

"I guess I was making sure everything's good. It's cool to chat with you once in a while, you know?"

117

There was a long pause, and then she typed again.

"Don't you get it? You're being needy," she said.

"What are you talking about? I'm trying to be nice."

"No. You're showing off that you're in Europe and trying to make yourself feel less lonely. You don't recognize it, but it's sad, and it's needy."

Bass tossed the phone down and stared at the table, feeling like someone had punched him in the face. He looked out at the surrounding plaza. A family with three girls walked past. The two older girls had super curly hair, and the youngest had wavy blond hair which glowed in the sun. The dad recorded a video with his phone while the mom stopped to look over the cafe menu.

A couple near him sat next to each other—holding hands, laughing, and kissing. Bass looked away.

His phone chimed with another text.

"Look, that's cool you're in Europe but you need to get your head in the game. You have a business to grow and you've got to clear up whatever's happening to you. Get a therapist if you need to."

Bass clenched his fist and pounded the table, his mind racing. She knew he wasn't a slacker. She knew how hard he worked. What bothered him the most, however, was how she struck a nerve. He didn't want to admit it, but Bass knew she was right—there was something broken inside.

She was typing another message.

"I hope you have fun, but don't text me to show off. Bye Bass."

He looked at the croissant, but lost his appetite. He left some money and walked away.

It was cold now, anyway.

CHAPTER TWENTY-FIVE

"Whoa!" a woman yelled.

Bass looked to where the sound was coming from and saw a woman splashing around in a fountain. He sat on the grass near the Jardins du Trocadéro, eating a baguette and looking out towards the Eiffel tower. JP went off somewhere to buy a couple of crepes.

"Whoa! Whoa!" the lady cried out repeatedly. She was making a huge scene, thrashing her arms, and sending water everywhere. She kept standing up and falling back into the fountain. Bass glanced around, but nobody else seemed to notice. When he glanced back at her, he realized she was looking directly at him.

She yelled louder.

"Whoa! Maybe someone will help me. I keep slipping in this fountain. Somebody please help me."

Bass tried to ignore her by looking away. *What a wacko*, he thought.

"Oh no, I fell down again. If only some young, handsome surfer dude from Huntington Beach named Bassy would save me."

Bass jerked his head back to look at the woman. "Rebekah?"

SEAN MARSHALL

"The one and only!"

Rebekah stopped splashing around and floated out of the fountain, towards him on the grass. She snapped her fingers and her clothes dried instantly. She wore a white shirt with blue horizontal stripes, red bell-bottom jeans pulled high on her waist, complete with a red scarf around her neck.

"I didn't recognize you without your crazy hair. Are you supposed to be from the 70s or something?"

"Almost," she said. Her red hair was still wet and hanging down. She snapped her fingers again and her hair poofed out as usual. "And now for the final touch..." She snapped again and a red beret materialized and landed gently on top of her hair.

"You like hats, don't you?"

"I like fashion! And yes, only the bold dare wear hats."

"Not a fan of the white clothing your fellow angels like to wear?"

"Oh Bassy, white has its place. But really, white has nothing on this little gem of an outfit. Classic French, circa 1978."

"I'm no expert, but that looks like an American trying to be French."

"Oh, what do you know?" Rebekah walked over to Bass and glanced at his baguette sandwich.

"Catch me up, Bassy," she said. "I haven't seen you since that little get-together in your office. Don't you love Paris so much?"

"Yeah, it's cool I suppose. Oh wait, except for the fact that I'm not sure what's happening with Jen and my business and I'm pretty sure Brittany hates me."

"Why do you think Brittany hates you?"

"I sent her a text yesterday. I probably shouldn't have. But I don't know, I figured maybe there's something still there."

Rebekah suddenly looked more serious than normal. "Walk with me."

"I can't leave here. JP will be coming back."

"Oh, we won't go far."

120

They moseyed up the hill towards the Musée National de la Marine. Bass pulled out his phone and put his hands-free in.

"Do you think anybody living in a big city hasn't seen a crazy person talking to themselves?"

"I'm not crazy," he said quickly, leaving his hands-free in. "I've got to ask you this, you're the love angel, right?"

"Of course I am," Rebekah said as she spun around on one toe.

"Can you tell me if there's something there? Like, with Brittany? If not her, is there someone else out there for me?"

"Why do you ask? I thought you were Mr. I'm-selling-my-business-man?"

Bass looked down. He realized his words revealed too much. It was almost impossible to be traveling around Europe, especially a city like Paris, and not think about having someone in his life. Every couple that walked past only seemed to mock his deeper feeling of being alone. If he had to admit it, he kept himself focused on his business because it was easier than dealing with what was stirring inside.

Something was working on him, though. The dream about the girl and his parents, the girl he saw in London, being in Paris —all of it swirled around in his soul.

"Yes, I am Mr. Selling-my-business-man or whatever, but I don't know. Maybe there's more to it all. Just yesterday, Mary was lecturing me about finding happiness. I've always thought I can worry about that later. I mean, I'm almost there."

Rebekah nodded and walked quietly next to Bass.

"Also, I had a dream a while back about a girl. I couldn't see her face but I really liked the way I felt with her. My mom and dad were there, too."

"Were they?" she asked and spun again on her toe. "That's interesting. What did you like about the girl?"

"I don't know. I mean, it was a dream. If I had to say one

thing, it would be her energy. I just felt whole with her —complete."

"And did you feel that way with Brittany?"

Bass looked down at the pavement, racing through his memories of Brittany. Without looking up, he answered, "Not really. No."

"Then why are you reaching out to her?"

He ran his hand through his hair and didn't want to answer. Brittany already told him. He was needy and lonely, and thinking about it made him feel weak. He stopped walking. Rebekah stopped also, but waited for Bass to speak.

"I don't know," he finally whispered.

Rebekah spoke softly, but deliberately. "I think you do but it's scary to admit, especially to yourself."

Bass heard laughter and turned to see a group of children chasing bubbles. He looked back towards the Eiffel Tower, which dominated the landscape.

"Let's turn back to where you were," Rebekah said. "JP is coming back."

"Well? What angelic wisdom do you have for me?"

"Oh, I've got some wisdom for you all right, Bassy. But first, you need to understand that love, true love, is the opposite of fear."

"I don't get it."

"These thoughts you're having, the ones that would drive you to text an ex-girlfriend, they're all based on fear. To be ready for love—amazing, happy, fulfilling, true love—you need to shed your fear."

"OK…how do I do that?"

"Through action!"

"Huh?"

"Check this out. I'm going to drop a wisdom bomb on you. Are you ready?"

Bass nodded.

A COUNCIL OF ANGELS

"Fear is cured by taking action. Taking action on behalf of others is called service. Service leads to love. Love leads to what Mary calls happiness. I call it your happily ever after."

Rebekah stopped walking, faced Bass directly. "You either live in fear or you live in love. It's your decision which." Then she made an explosion motion with her hand and said in a deep voice, "Boom!"

"Huh? How does that help me know if there's a chance with Brittany?"

"Oh Bassy, you're smart enough to piece it together. But I promise it goes hand-in-hand with everything else that my heavenly amigos have already shared with you."

She then leaned in closer, cupped her hand, and whispered, "You either live in fear or you live in love. It's your decision which. Your happily ever after is completely up to you." She backed away and twirled back up the path.

"There," she said, almost shouting, "you chew on that for a while. Once it makes sense to you, your whole life will change."

She twirled farther and farther away.

Bass yelled after her. "Will it help me find my treasure?"

Rebekah simply giggled and disappeared.

CHAPTER TWENTY-SIX

Bass and JP arrived in Barcelona on a late flight out of Paris. They checked into their hotel, located near La Rambla.

JP collapsed onto his bed while Bass opened his laptop to check his email. He skipped through most of the emails, but one caught his eye. It was from Kathy. He clicked on it.

Hi Bass,

I hope you're having fun in Europe! JP sent me your itinerary. I'm so jealous. So much history! I hope you get this in time but while you're in Germany, see if you can go to a place called Heidelberg. From the map, I can tell it's quite a ways from Berlin, though.

I've been doing some research into my own family history and we've got some ancestors from there. It's really interesting. I'm thinking I might need to do my own European vacation soon. Maybe you'll come with me?

Anyway, thought I would tell you I'm going to see a specialist about my heart. Actually, my boss is making me do it after she saw me get a bit dizzy after my heart did one of its jumping jacks. Everything is fine though.

Well, I hope you have fun on your vacation. You've needed one for a while. JP wasn't shy in saying you're looking for girls over there. Call it a mother's hunch, but I think you'll meet someone nice very soon.

Love you,
Mom

His eyes were heavy as he closed the laptop. The clock said 2:13 a.m. He looked over to JP, who hadn't bothered to change out of his clothes and was already snoring loudly.

Bass hit the light switch and rolled over in his bed. His last thought was hoping his mother was right. He wanted to meet someone very soon.

CHAPTER TWENTY-SEVEN

The sun shone brightly, and the beautiful city of Barcelona was warming up. It was full of art, stunning architecture, and Bass loved listening to the locals speak their native Catalan language. It wasn't hard to notice how proud they were of their unique culture. As he identified with their spirit of independence, he also felt a sense of pride, even though he'd only been there for less than a day.

When Bass and JP left their hotel, they walked past the Santa Caterina market, which Bass thought was the most unique and beautiful market he'd ever seen. They filled two large bags with fresh bread, deli meats of all kinds, and various cheeses and then sat down outside the market to gorge themselves.

JP kept saying, "Mmm…." every time he took a bite. "Try this one!" he said over and over as he picked through the assorted cheeses they bought. "Try this meat. The guy said it had sheep blood in it."

"Sheep blood?" Bass asked. The word blood made him think about his toe.

"Or was it goat's blood?" JP said. "I don't know. I know he said 'sang' and I'm pretty sure that means blood. You know, like 'sangre'. You're the Mexican here. You should know that."

"Half-Mexican. And besides, you know I don't speak much Spanish."

"Your last name is literally Martinez, and you live in Southern California. Your ancestors would be ashamed of you."

JP laughed, but at some level, Bass knew he was right. Even Kathy, his mother who came from mostly German ancestry, knew more Spanish than he did. Bass thought she would love it if he told her he was going to take Spanish classes. She'd probably even use it as an excuse to get him to learn more about his family.

After they stuffed themselves with as much bread, meat, and cheese as they could handle, they headed towards La Sagrada Familia. As they walked past a corner of the market, Bass noticed a homeless man ahead of them. It wasn't the first homeless person he'd seen in Europe, but something about this guy stood out.

The man sat with his back against the wall, knees up and tucked in, head down, with one of his hands extended. In front of where he sat was a cardboard sign which read, "Ajuda'm si us plau." Below that, "Help me please" in English.

He said nothing but simply sat there with his hand stretched out, his palm facing the sky. Something about his presence struck Bass. It was his apparent humility. Bass remembered what Rebekah said in Paris about helping others. He took ten euros from the cash JP gave him earlier and put it in the man's hand as they walked past. He didn't look up but said, "Thank you" in English.

After they passed the man, JP said, "I think it's nice of you to give *my* money to poor people." He could barely finish the sentence before laughing at his own joke.

"I know. Sorry. I mean, thanks. Seriously, I'm good for it."

"I know you are. Duh. And you're a rich boy so I'm going to charge you interest."

"Hilarious. But I'm not rich yet."

"I hear the words coming out of your mouth but your fancy house and your Range Rover are saying something different."

"Whatever."

As they walked towards La Sagrada Familia, something about the man pulled at Bass and he couldn't stop thinking about him. He wondered what Mary would say. Jacob probably would have said that Bass should have given him a high five or something. Rebekah probably would have told him to say "I love you" or do a funny dance to cheer him up.

He felt guilty, like he should have done something more. As they walked up the street, the next block opened to a park and they could see La Sagrada Familia behind it. At first glance, it was impressive, and the closer they got, the more detail they saw. It was not only a church, it was a work of art.

As they approached the cathedral, they noticed a small deli market. They grabbed a couple of sodas to quench their thirst and sat down on a bench, which looked directly up at the stunning building. Bass's feet throbbed, and he stared down at them, noticing his toenail was still cut in half but didn't hurt. He pulled his shorts up a bit and looked at his leg. The scabs were almost gone and he would have a faint but cool looking scar. He thought about the accident. It seemed forever ago. He thought about the drunk driver.

What was he doing right now? Is he OK? he wondered.

"Dude, I'm not doing that walk again," JP said. He guzzled his soda in one gulp and let out an enormous burp. Some people walking past stared at Bass. He punched JP—less to hurt JP and more to show the people it wasn't him that burped.

"That was a lot of walking," JP said. "It didn't look that far on the map. This place is bigger than I realized."

"Yeah, but it's a cool city."

"What's been your favorite place so far?"

"I liked London a lot. Berlin? Meh. Paris was cool. So many

A COUNCIL OF ANGELS

bridges and beautiful buildings." Bass paused and looked around. "I think Barcelona is my favorite. I just like the *feel* of it."

"Dude, wait until we get to Italy. You're gonna freaking love it!"

After their sodas, they waited forever in line to do the tour but were glad they did. The building was even more impressive on the inside. They took the metro back, but Bass headed to the exit before their stop, telling JP he'd meet him at the hotel.

JP raised an eyebrow. "What are you going to do?"

"I want to check out that market one more time."

JP shrugged. "Whatever floats your boat."

Bass got off at the Urquinaona stop and made his way to the market. He turned the corner and sure enough, the homeless man was still there. He had no idea what he was going to do, but he knew the angels would probably be proud if he helped somehow.

He sat down next to the man, who moved his head a little. Bass said nothing at first and watched a few people pass by. One lady looked at Bass, looked at the man, and then back at Bass, trying to figure out what was happening.

Bass finally spoke. "Hablas Español?"

The man replied, "I speak English, too."

"I wanted to see if there's something I can do to help you."

"I do not need your help." The man moved his face and for the first time, Bass saw his eyes. They were yellow and bloodshot. His pupils were dark, almost black. "I do not want your help."

"Can I get you a place to stay, or at least a warm meal?"

The man repeated, but more forcefully, "I do not want your help!"

"Geez! OK man. Chill. I'm just trying to help but, whatever." Bass couldn't believe the guy's attitude. He didn't want to help a man who was content to sit there all day doing nothing but begging. He started with the best of intentions, but his quick temper got the better of him.

129

Bass stood and said, "It's a waste, you know. It's a waste of a life to squat here doing what you do."

The man said nothing. He didn't even move.

Bass clenched his fists but looked around the plaza. He felt like someone was watching and thought it might be the angels. He turned to walk away but stopped, closed his eyes, and ran a hand through his hair. He let out a sigh, knowing what he had to do. He walked back and put his hand on the man's shoulder, but the man didn't move.

"I'm sorry for what I said. I don't know what you've gone through. I have no idea." Bass wanted to say more, something really meaningful, but couldn't think of anything. He just lifted his hand and walked away.

Instead of taking the metro back to the hotel, Bass walked the rest of the way. He thought about every time he'd helped someone up to this point. It wasn't the happy, feel-good stuff from the movies. It felt like a waste of energy. And where were the angels, anyway? And was he even getting any closer to finding his treasure?

Bass said out loud, "Hey council of angels people. If you guys can hear me, I think this is all a waste. I'm quitting, OK? I'm gonna do what I want to do. If you can hear me, just leave me alone. I don't need your help. I got this."

He passed a small cafe where a dozen people sat at tables sipping on coffee, smoking, and reading newspapers. Once he passed them, he continued. "I've always been alone. My dad died when I was a kid. My mom always worked. I'm fine. I don't need anyone's help. You hear me?"

Bass stopped talking, swallowed hard, and gritted his teeth. He blinked forcibly to stem the tears that crept into the corners of his eyes. He sniffed hard and walked faster towards the hotel. The last thing he wanted was to be seen talking to himself and crying.

CHAPTER TWENTY-EIGHT

Skylar sat down on some steps of a building, looking back at the corner of the market, and opened her bag of goodies. She had some dried fruit and about 10 different kinds of olives. Amazed at the selection, she couldn't decide on just one, so she ended up buying as many as would fit in her backpack.

She grabbed the first cup of olives and popped a couple into her mouth. In an instant, she was delighted by the deep, rich, salty flavors.

This is heaven right here, she thought.

She sat back against the building and surveyed the people walking by the market. She noticed a homeless man sitting with his hand extended outward. As Skylar watched, she saw a guy, obviously an American, walk up and sit down next to the homeless man. She stopped chewing her olives and gazed intently, wondering what he was doing.

The American said something, but the homeless man hardly moved. He threw his hands in the air and said something else even louder. Then he stood up and walked away, looking upset.

What was he doing? Skylar thought.

A moment later, she watched as the guy came back and put a

hand on the homeless man's shoulder. His body language was calmer, humbled even. She desperately wished she could have heard what he was saying. He lingered for a moment and then walked away. He looked defeated with his head hung low, shoulders slumped, and staring at the ground.

She kept her eyes on him until he eventually turned the corner. He was young, probably around her same age. And he was handsome. He was too far away, but something about him was familiar, like she'd seen him before.

Skylar looked back to the homeless man, who remained unchanged. She glanced back down to her bag of olives and decided to save them for later. What just happened was too interesting.

Who was that guy? What did he say, and why was he sad?

CHAPTER TWENTY-NINE

"Sooner or later, you're going to have to face that young man," Nancy said. She and Dan sat at the kitchen table in their house in Fountain Valley, California. It was covered with folders and letters, and Nancy had a calculator in front of her and a pencil in her hand.

"I know," Dan said. "It scares me to death."

"We can handle everything else—the court, the attorney fees, and so on, but that's the one thing we can't write a check for."

It hurt Dan to hear that. Nancy had to pick up extra hours at her job to pay off the mess he'd gotten them into. In the last month since the accident, they also used up a good chunk of their limited savings to pay for everything.

Dan knew she was right. He would have to face the young man he hit. He would have to ask for forgiveness. He didn't want to do it, but he knew it was the correct thing to do. He'd been broken. He lost his job and caused an accident on the same day. And yet, she stood by him. Suddenly, he was overwhelmed with a feeling of gratitude for his wife.

He took her hand and said, "You're right. I will talk to that boy." His chest constricted, and he struggled to speak. "Thank

SEAN MARSHALL

you so much for standing by me. I know I don't say it much, but I...I love you."

Nancy put down her pencil and looked up at Dan. She paused for a moment, searching for what to say. When she spoke, she simply said, "I love you, too."

CHAPTER THIRTY

"La margherita per favore," JP said, trying his best at an Italian accent to the server taking the order.

Bass and JP sat at a table outside at a small cafe in Rome with the entire Roman Forum at their backs. After two full days in Barcelona, they finally arrived in Italy. Embarrassed by JP's horrible Italian accent, and also that he was ordering—of all things—pizza, Bass let out a huge sigh.

"Dude, we're in Italy! It seems silly to get pizza," Bass said.

"What? It's on the menu. It's not like they put this here just for American tourists. If they did, they'd have a Chicago deep dish or meat lover's or something. It's fine. Stop freaking out."

JP looked up at the server. "Umm, excuse me, uh, scusi, due margherita per favore. I'm hungry," he said, pointing at his stomach.

Bass pointed to a dish on the menu that said *tortelli di brasato* and said, "grazie."

"Excellent. Thank you, gentlemen," the server replied in perfect English.

JP looked at Bass and blurted out, "Oops!" and laughed. He pulled out his phone and scrolled through his photos.

135

Bass looked around, taking in his surroundings. Everything about Italy astounded him—the architecture, the food, the people.

The language impressed him the most. He absolutely loved listening to the Italians speak. It sounded like music. He wondered if his mom would be upset if he chose to learn Italian instead of Spanish. He then imagined her telling him that he has ancestors from Italy as well.

He looked over at a couple at the table next to them. The man had salt and pepper hair with a salt and pepper goatee. The woman was blond and wore a brown leather jacket. They worked their way through a shared bowl of gnocchi. They said nothing, but smiled at each other as they ate.

A few minutes passed by and the server brought the food. Bass took a bite of his tortelli and couldn't believe how good it tasted.

JP lifted a piece of his pizza and offered it to Bass. "You want a little tastaroo?"

"Yeah, might as well."

Bass reached over to grab the slice right as an older lady came walking up with her hand out, begging. He ignored her. JP stared at him incredulously for a second before reaching into his own pocket. He gave the woman some coins, and she whispered something back in Italian.

After she left, JP asked, "Are you out of cash? I can give you more."

"No. I'm done doing stuff for other people," Bass said.

"That's a weird thing to say."

"Whatever."

JP stared at his friend for a moment and looked like he was going to say something. Instead, he thought better of it and shoved an entire slice of pizza into his mouth.

Bass picked at the rest of his meal. After they finished, JP paid the server, and they headed to the Roman Forum. As they

A COUNCIL OF ANGELS

got closer, JP increased his pace until he was practically skipping.

"Can you believe this was the heart of the Roman Empire? Caesar walked here! And they had crazy death matches right over there," JP said, pointing over to the colosseum. They were going there the next day on an official guided tour that JP already booked.

"You know what would make this even better?" JP asked. "Gelato! I'm going to get some. What flavor do you want?"

"Umm, chocolate. No wait. Strawberry. If they have it."

"One strawberry gelato coming right up, sir," he said as he turned and jogged off.

"Be sure not to drop it!" Bass shouted after him. JP didn't look back, but shook a fist at him in the air.

Bass touched one of the pillars and was impressed to think how old they were. He wished he could go back in time to see what it really looked like.

"Rome was truly amazing to behold," a man said, standing next to Bass. He turned and saw Jacob wearing a white toga with a laurel wreath on his bald head. "When they say empire, they weren't kidding."

"Hey, not sure if you got my message, but I'm done with this whole angel thing," Bass said. "You're never there when I really need you and all this heavenly advice you've given me hasn't worked out at all."

"What do you mean?"

Bass looked out at the people walking around. He pulled out his hands-free as usual and walked down the path among the Foro di Cesare.

"Look, thank you for what you guys are trying to do, whatever that is, but I'm good. I already know what I want. I don't need your help."

Jacob was quiet for a moment, waiting to see if Bass had anything more to say.

137

"Is that it?"

"Yeah, you guys can go help someone else. I got this."

Jacob smiled and said, "You didn't really think it would be that easy, did you? That you could throw a couple of coins at a man and you're done?"

"What do you mean?"

"Look sport, we're serious when we say we'll help you find your life's greatest treasure, but it's going to take some *work* on your part."

"Yeah, but the more I try to serve or whatever, it just ends up feeling like a waste of time. I was fine before. I had my life on track. I can do this on my own. I always have."

Jacob looked down at the colosseum, and Bass followed his gaze.

"You know the expression, 'Rome wasn't built in a day'?"

"Yeah, I've heard that."

"What if I told you that your dream life isn't built by wanting to make it happen but actually *doing* the steps to make it happen?"

"I don't get it."

"Go this way."

They turned and walked towards the colosseum.

"Here's the deal, output equals input. If you want to have a great life, a fantastic life, you need to do the stuff that's going to get you there. And we've already told you what that is."

"Serving others?" Bass asked with a voice full of attitude. "Yeah, no thank you. It doesn't work for me."

"Have you ever gone surfing in really huge waves?"

"You mean like the day you almost killed me? Yes, I have."

Jacob grinned, proud of what he did. "Good, now think about trying to paddle out through those sets. It's hard, right?"

Bass thought about it for a minute, but really had to concentrate. He was standing in the middle of Rome, trying to

A COUNCIL OF ANGELS

picture surfing in California. But Jacob was right. Paddling through a set of big waves can be exhausting.

"But then what happens once you get past the oncoming waves?"

"You wait for the next set," Bass said.

"And?"

"You pick your wave and go for it."

"And?"

"And what? You have an awesome ride."

"Better than a day where the waves are flat?"

"Obviously."

"That's the point. The greater the struggle, the greater the reward." Jacob looked up to the colosseum and said again, "Output equals input. Just like that monster building over there, big, long-lasting stuff doesn't happen overnight. You've got to work at it, tiger."

"Yes, cool. I get that. But I already told you this. Every time I help someone, it doesn't work. It even backfires on me. It's like," Bass searched for the words, "negative karma or something."

"Are you upset about that man in Barcelona?"

Bass nodded.

"What did you expect?"

"I don't know. I was trying to be cool. I figured he'd like another human actually talking with him instead of just giving him spare change. In fact, I gave him ten euros. And that's money I'm borrowing from JP!"

"Would you consider that a good deed?"

"Yes," Bass replied.

"Then that should be enough, right? A good deed is never wasted. That guy benefited from your actions. And I've got a pretty good feeling, you'll also benefit from those actions. You might not see it immediately but that's not the point."

Bass thought he saw Jacob's eyes flash. For a moment, his

139

light-colored eyes seemed to flash white, as if they were alive. But something still bothered him.

"What is the point, then?" he said.

"The point is to serve," Jacob replied.

"I did."

"Yes, but you were hoping for some kind of reaction. You wanted him to do something back for you."

"Yeah, so?"

Jacob sat down on one of the railings running along the ruins. He patted the railing next to him to get Bass to sit down. Bass sat on the metal bar, but it was uncomfortable. He wondered how Jacob, as big as he was, could even balance, let alone be comfortable.

"When you serve, you need to stop thinking about what's in it for you. It should be enough that you did something for someone else. That's it, plain and simple."

"But I thought you guys said that happiness comes to those who serve?"

"Oh, it comes all right."

Bass sighed. "OK, look then, I told you guys. I'm good. I can handle this on my own. Thanks."

"You don't get off that easy there, champ. We've got more good things in store for you. You'll like it, I promise. Besides, we're only what, twelve days into this whole treasure thing? Give it some time."

Jacob smiled and stood up. "Your BFF is coming. Looks like they didn't have strawberry."

JP moved down the path, holding two cups, and leaned down to lick his gelato as he walked. He saw Bass and held up the other cup. It was chocolate.

"Hey," Jacob said, "I'll give you a little clue about happiness. Think about JP. Think about everything he's done ever since your accident. You can go back even further if you like. That guy

A COUNCIL OF ANGELS

understands happiness." Jacob paused and looked at JP, who was getting close. "Before I go, think about this, time spent serving others is never wasted. JP gets it. Now it's your turn."

April 30, 6:00 a.m.

Greetings Team,

Thank you all so much for everything you've said and done so far. I think you're getting under Bass's skin, in a good way!

I sure hope we can reach him. I know you're all aware of his recent change of heart. I'm not sure if we're really helping him make progress. Please, I don't want to lose him. I can't. Not again.

Mary, you're up next. Do what you do best. Please. There's still so much that needs to happen. I've been informed that I also get to increase my own influence with him. I hope I can say and do the right things.

I've learned now that even angels need to have faith. I believe in this council. I believe in Bass. Everything so far has brought us to this point. I'll help the best I can.

Warm Regards,
  Michael

CHAPTER THIRTY-ONE

Bass reached into his pocket to grab his phone, but when he removed it, something else dropped to the ground. He bent down and picked up the card he received from the woman on the tube in London. On it was the quote from Henry David Thoreau. He read it out loud.

"Could a greater miracle take place than for us to look through each other's eyes for an instant?"

JP turned his head towards Bass. "What'd you say?"

"Oh, nothing."

He thought about the quote for a moment and looked around. They were in the middle of Piazza di San Pietro. It was late afternoon on their second day in Rome and the sun was already dropping in the sky. JP spun slowly in a circle with his phone, trying to take a panoramic shot.

What would it be like to see through these people's eyes, Bass thought.

"I can show you something similar," said a female voice next to Bass. It was Mary. She was in her usual white clothing, but this time wore a red bandana in her hair.

Bass raised his eyebrows and asked, "You can?"

A COUNCIL OF ANGELS

"What'd you say?" JP asked, not taking his eyes off of his phone.

"Nothing," Bass said.

"Stop doing that!"

Bass couldn't help but laugh. He caught Mary covering a smile with her hand.

"Hey, before we go into the church, I need to get off my feet for a minute. We've been walking all day," Bass said, pointing to a fountain nearby. "I'm gonna sit over there, OK?"

"Cool, cool. I'm trying to get a sweet 360 shot of this plaza. It's hard to keep my hands steady the entire time. I keep messing up the lines."

Bass walked over to the fountain with Mary at his side.

"How are you Sebastian? How do you feel?"

"A little tired. Why? What's up?"

"I'll get straight to the point. Today, I'm going to give you a very special gift. Please have a seat."

"What do you mean?"

"Trust me," she said. "Now, sit down and close your eyes."

He sat on the edge of the fountain and lowered his eyelids. Mary looked up to the sky for a moment and then reached out to Bass. He opened one eye and said, "What are you doing?"

"Close your eyes and try to let go of everything. Right now, it's just you and me. Take a deep breath and relax."

Bass closed his eyes, bowed his head, and inhaled deeply through his nose. Suddenly, he felt two warm hands resting delicately on his eyelids. He wanted to speak but couldn't. He wanted to open his eyes, but didn't. He knew they were Mary's hands.

How could it be? he wondered.

He could actually *feel* her hands. They lingered for just a moment and then she said, "Sebastian, open your eyes."

Bass did so and saw Mary directly in front of him. She was radiant—brighter than he'd ever seen her. Her clothing glowed, but they paled compared to her skin and especially her eyes. He

145

looked into them, but couldn't understand what was happening. They were moving somehow. It almost appeared as if they were on fire. Or rather, that there were small fires inside her eyes.

A glow emanated from her and seemed brighter than even the sun. He couldn't look away, yet it didn't hurt his eyes.

"What you see, Sebastian, is my light."

"Your light?"

"Yes, I've given you a special gift. It's the ability to see others the way God sees them. Now, look around you."

Bass stared at the hundreds of people walking through the plaza. They all had lights that emanated from their bodies. Some were dazzling and others very dim, almost nonexistent. Bass was captivated by everyone he saw.

A lone guy around his same age walked towards him. They caught eyes for a moment. In an instant, Bass felt he knew everything about the guy, but his light wasn't very strong. Bass felt a surge of emotions—apprehension, surprise, disappointment, even fear. He moved past but shot a look back, so Bass gave him a quick wave. The guy just nodded his head and kept moving.

"Now, look at the children," Mary said.

Bass focused on the kids in the plaza. He focused on a small boy holding hands with his father. His light was shining brightly as he stared up at his dad with a smile.

Bass looked towards another small family walking near the fountain. There was a girl pushing a stroller with a baby boy in it, and they both shimmered. The mother glowed, but the father's light was far less bright. In fact, it was almost dark. As Bass concentrated on him, he could understand everything the man was thinking. He felt fear. It was a concern about money. The father looked at the baby in the stroller and Bass understood. Everything flooded into his mind at once.

The baby's health was in jeopardy, and the father was the only one that knew. He recently checked an email that showed some test results. They were not good. The problem could be fixed, but

A COUNCIL OF ANGELS

it would take time and it would be expensive. Bass experienced the full weight of what the father was feeling as the family slowly moved past.

The more Bass looked around, the more he realized that most of the bright lights came from the children in the plaza.

"Many of them have not yet been dimmed by the negative influences of the world," Mary said. "Their lights are pure."

Bass stood up to get a better look. He fixated on an old couple sitting next to each other, holding hands, their lights glowing brightly.

"Sebastian, what do you think? What do you see?"

Bass tried to speak, but nothing came out. Anytime he focused on a single person, he could instantly feel their hopes and dreams, but also their fears and problems. He felt an overwhelming desire to help all of them. Although it wasn't normally his nature, he wanted to give them all hugs and words of cheer.

"I..." Bass started, "I can't describe it. There's a lot of light. But it looks like there's also a lot of pain. I want to help."

Bass looked back at Mary, who smiled with her hands folded in front of her.

"I'll give you a clue," she said. "One word. It starts with an 's.'"

"Serve?"

Mary nodded.

Bass looked back out to the plaza and couldn't believe the array of lights before him. It looked like the entire place was shining. He was also astounded to realize how many people's lights were barely lit, flickering almost.

"Sebastian, as you can see, everyone has light. It radiates happiness and love. Some have less but everyone has it. Like adding another log to the fire, you can help that light burn brighter."

Mary sat down next to Bass on the fountain and gazed out at the people walking around.

"Can you see how everyone is so special to God? Can you see how everyone has so much potential?"

Bass shook his head and threw his arms in the air. "What am I supposed to do? Go around helping everyone?"

"It's your job to do what you can, when you can."

Bass stared at the ground and pondered her words for a moment. When he looked up, the lights around the people began to fade.

"What's happening?"

"You've been given a glimpse of what God sees. It's the potential of every human soul. It's a tremendous gift, but it's only temporary to help you on your way. It's sort of like an object lesson, if you will."

Bass continued looking around the plaza. There were so many people, so many different stories, so many feelings.

"There are a lot of people on this earth. Where will you start?"

Bass didn't need to think. "That poor dad with the sick baby."

"Just him?"

"Well, yes," Bass said slowly. "I guess...start with the people whose lights aren't shining as brightly?"

Mary smiled. "I think you're getting it."

"But how? When I can't see people's lights anymore, how do I know who to help?"

"You've got to feel it, Sebastian. Try to look people in the eyes and smile. Make it a habit. It will be a tool for you to know who to help. You'll be able to see it in their eyes."

Bass glanced to the family slowly walking away.

"I've got to do something," he said. He ran over to JP, who was still spinning around in a circle, trying to keep his hands steady.

"JP, I need all the cash you have in your wallet!"

"Steady, steady," JP said as he spun. "There, nailed it." He looked up at Bass. "Why?"

"Please! I need all the cash you have. Hurry!"

JP reached for his wallet, pulled out 310 euros, and handed it to Bass.

"Give me those dollars too."

"What? Why? I'm happy to help, but what the heck are you doing?"

"Just trust me. I'm good for it."

"You said that already," JP said. He gave Bass another 100 dollars.

Bass ran over to the family and tapped on the man's shoulder and said, "Sir, excuse me...umm...scusi..."

The man looked confused. His daughter stood next to him and looked up at Bass and smiled.

Bass said, "Do you speak English?"

The man shook his head no. Bass extended his hand and held out the cash. The man looked at it and shook his head no again, clearly not understanding. Bass pointed at the baby and then at the cash.

"This money, for your baby," he said.

The man shook his head no again, this time more emphatically. The woman looked apprehensive and moved the stroller away, grabbing the girl's hand.

Oh no, they're misunderstanding! Bass thought.

He panicked. Bass pointed to the baby again and then pointed to his own lungs. "Your baby. Lungs. Sick." He made a coughing noise. "Please take this." He tried to hand the man the cash again.

The woman stopped moving and looked at her husband, desperately trying to figure out what was happening. The man stared at Bass intently, trying to understand what he was doing. Bass gave a weak smile and tried to push the cash into the man's hand.

The man shook his head as tears welled up in his eyes. He looked at his wife, the baby, and then back at Bass. The man blinked forcefully and pursed his lips. Bass insisted again and pushed the cash into the man's hand and pointed at the baby.

"Please," Bass said. "Per favore. Take this."

He used both hands, one to take the man's hand and the other to put the cash in it. He closed the man's hand over the cash.

"Per favore," Bass said and took a step backwards.

The man's eyes bored into Bass's for a second. He shook his head in disbelief and then lunged forward, pulling Bass into a tight hug. Bass felt like he was lifting off the ground, and he blinked fast to hold the tears back. The man released him but held him by the shoulders.

"Grazie. Grazie mille."

Bass nodded and backed away. He wiped his eyes with his shirt, swallowed hard, and sniffed to clear his nose to regain his composure. He gave the family a wave and turned back towards JP.

After walking about twenty yards, he looked back to see the woman talking to the man. Clearly upset, she was flailing her arms and speaking loudly. Bass watched the man say something back while pointing to the baby. She listened, and then reached down to the baby, picked him up, and held him tight. Bass hoped he hadn't caused any problems.

"What was that all about?" JP asked. "Wait, dude, are you crying?"

"No," Bass lied.

JP examined Bass closer and a wide grin slowly formed across his face.

Bass quickly offered an explanation. "I don't know, I just felt like I needed to give that family some money." He looked toward their hotel, trying to change the subject. "Do you have any more cash in the hotel?"

"No, but I can always take more out. But," JP said, "I'm only going to take out twenty euros at a time. I don't mind you giving money to people, but I can't help all of Europe!"

They both laughed.

A COUNCIL OF ANGELS

JP stopped laughing as he looked over Bass's shoulder. "Umm...dude?"

Bass felt a pull on his arm. He turned to see the woman staring at him with tears streaming down her face, smearing her mascara. She took Bass's arm and pulled him close, squeezing him in a tight hug. As she pulled away, she said, "Grazie," over and over again. Behind her, the little girl walked up and held out a bracelet. It was a silver chain with a tiny angel charm on it.

Bass knelt down to the girl's level. He shook his head. "Oh, no. I can't take that."

The girl looked up at her mom. The woman took the bracelet and put it into Bass's hand. She closed his hand over it the same way he'd done moments before with her husband. She took his other hand, lifted him up, and hugged him again, this time even tighter. She backed away slightly but put a finger on his chest and said, "Angel. You."

Bass could hardly stand. His knees quivered. His chest clamped down and he fought hard to speak. "Grazie," he squeaked out. He took a deep breath and looked back at the girl. "What is your name?"

The girl looked confused, so he pointed at himself and said, "Bass." Then he pointed at her and said, "Your name?"

The mom said, "Isabella."

Bass cupped his hands in a prayer position and said, "Grazie, Isabella. Grazie."

The little girl smiled and took her mother's hand. The family slowly turned and walked away as the girl looked over her shoulder and waved at Bass. He quickly waved back.

Bass carefully put the tiny angel bracelet into his pocket and then glanced over at JP, who stood stiffly, like he was in shock. His eyebrows were raised, his eyes wide, and his mouth was open. Then slowly, he started to nod his head approvingly as the corners of his mouth stretched into a smile.

He simply said, "Dude."

CHAPTER THIRTY-TWO

I have to jump in here and say that as an angel, it's exciting when we see people begin to change. It's thrilling, actually. It was clear that Bass's experience in Rome made a tremendous impact on him and things were changing for him.

At this point, I was also given permission to get more involved. I can't quite put it into words how grateful I was to share this time with him. OK, back to the report.

The next morning, Bass and JP boarded a train leaving Rome and headed to Venice. Bass spent the entire ride playing out the previous day's experience over and over in his mind. He thought about everyone he saw. He thought especially of the family and hoped the baby would be OK.

For the first time in a long time, he said a prayer. "Dear God," he muttered under his breath so JP couldn't hear him, "if you're really listening, please take care of that family. Please help that baby."

As Bass gazed out the window, he was mesmerized by the beauty of the Italian countryside. Stone pines and cypress trees dotted the grassy green hills. Now and then, Bass saw small towns made up of stone houses with red tile roofs. The streets were made of cobblestone. He saw fields of vineyards with workers tending to the grapes.

Everything he witnessed seemed magical. He couldn't tell if it was because of what happened to him or if it was because the country was so beautiful.

As they were getting close to Venice, Bass caught JP staring at him with a huge, cheesy grin.

"What?"

"What?" JP mimicked back.

"Whatever."

They arrived in the Stazione di Venezia Santa Lucia mid-morning. Bass grabbed his backpack and followed JP out of the station towards the city of Venice. When they got out of the doors, Bass thought he'd stepped onto a movie set. The buildings looked too beautiful to be real. In front of him stood the green dome of the church of San Simeon Piccolo with the main canal of the city passing in front. He knew the city had canals instead of roads, but he couldn't believe how beautiful it was in real life.

"Wow, wow, wow!" JP said. "Holy crap, this place is gorgeous!"

"I know," Bass said. "I can't stop smiling!"

The two slowly walked forward towards the canal. It was busy with small boats and water taxis moving about. A seagull cried overhead and reminded Bass that they were near the ocean.

This city is ON the ocean! Bass thought.

JP pulled out his phone. "My email says our hotel isn't far from here. Wanna just walk?"

"Let's do it," Bass replied.

The two headed towards the first main bridge into the city, the Ponte degli Scalzi. Suddenly, vendors practically surrounded them, pushing selfie-sticks into their faces.

"Ten euros! Ten euros!" they shouted.

JP said no to them and tried to push through. Bass looked into the eyes of the vendor closest to him. He was African, and Bass saw fear in the man's yellow-tinted eyes. Bass smiled and said, "Non, merci."

The man smiled back and made a bowing motion before backing up.

"I didn't know you spoke French," JP said. "And hello, we're in Italy. Not France."

"Yeah, yeah, whatever. I just felt like that's what I was supposed to say. I must have picked up some French in Paris or something. I don't know, maybe he speaks French."

Bass and JP finally reached their hotel and dropped off their packs. They asked the front desk clerk where the best restaurants were, and he directed them to a few places near Piazza San Marco. They thanked the clerk and made their way through the city.

It was unbelievable. They took pictures at almost every turn. It reminded Bass of a ride at Disneyland, though he couldn't say which. There was no beautiful Italian city ride there that he knew of. He thought something so amazing couldn't be real—it had to be some kind of theme park attraction. He saw a lady hanging her laundry on a line and reminded him that people did, in fact, live there.

They finally made it to one of the restaurants near Piazza San Marco. It was lunchtime, and the restaurant was crowded. They made their way to an open table when suddenly four Russian men cut in front of them and sat down.

"Dude, this was our table!" JP yelled.

Only one of the Russians even looked up. He had a buzz cut and blue eyes. He ignored JP completely and looked directly at Bass, challenging him. Bass removed his sunglasses and looked into the Russian's eyes. The other Russians glanced up.

Bass stared calmly, patted the Russian lightly on his shoulder, and smiled. He gave a little nod and then walked off. JP stood there for a second, his head swiveling between the Russians and

A COUNCIL OF ANGELS

Bass, who was now already leaving the restaurant. The best he could come up with was to point his finger at the Russians. They all laughed as he walked away, fuming.

He caught up to Bass and said, "What the heck, man? You let those guys bully their way to that table!"

"It's not worth it. There are a lot of places to eat here. Let's see what's up this way."

As they walked down one of the streets off the main plaza, they got caught in the crowd of people behind two ladies, both of whom were smoking. Bass waved his arms but wasn't bothered by the smoke.

A minute later, Bass and JP turned the corner and walked down an alley, but got cut off by a group of at least twenty Chinese tourists. The group seemed oblivious of anyone else, focused only on snapping photos with their smartphones. Bass and JP waited patiently for them to pass before moving forward.

JP stared at Bass in disbelief. "Something's changed in you, man. The old you would've gone off on all of those people. You just smiled at them. What the heck is going on?"

"I don't know," Bass said.

"I think that family in Rome changed you," JP said. "It's a good change," he added quickly. "I think 'ol JP was right in talking you into coming on this vacation." He gave himself a pat on the back.

Bass smiled and said, "Thank you, man. You were right. It's been a great trip."

They turned another corner and saw a small cafe with a view of the water, with plenty of seating.

"This looks good," JP said.

"Yeah, it's perfect," Bass added. "Way better than the restaurant those Russians are eating at."

"Yeah," JP said. "But first, I'm gonna look for a bathroom."

Bass sat down at an open table and looked towards the waterfront. A moment later, I appeared behind Bass and crossed in front of him.

155

"Is this seat taken?"

"Oh hey, Michael," Bass said. "I haven't seen much of you."

"It's mostly my job to record everything, but when the timing is right, I get to actually meet with you."

Bass pulled out his phone, pretending he was on a call.

"Can you believe this city? It's incredible!"

"I know. It's a magical place."

Bass turned his head almost sideways as he stared at me, looking at me as though he'd seen me before. Not before, like at the beach or his office, but from somewhere else. He smiled, and I could tell he was different. Mary's gift worked. He was happier. He was beginning to understand.

"Do you know what happened to me yesterday?"

"You mean in the plaza with Mary?"

"Yes."

"It's what we angels like to refer to as *true sight*," I said.

"True sight," Bass repeated out loud. "Yes, that makes sense. It makes total sense." Bass looked around at the people walking past. I could tell he was hoping to get the sight back again.

I sat forward in the chair, feeling an overwhelming surge of compassion for him. I wanted him to be able to keep true sight all the time. To see others as God sees them is truly a profound gift. Bass had to learn, though. Before I knew it, I blurted out, "There's more fun stuff ahead."

Bass turned back to me. "What do you mean?"

I hesitated. I didn't know how much I was allowed to say, but I figured they wouldn't let me know something and then appear to Bass if I couldn't share it myself. I played it safe, though.

"Well, with your treasure," I said, "you've started down the path. There's a lot more work to do but I can tell you there's a lot of good stuff still to come. Life-changing stuff."

Bass sat up in his chair.

"Better than true sight?"

I hesitated again. "It's different…but good."

A COUNCIL OF ANGELS

JP was making his way back, and I felt myself fading. Bass noticed it, too.

"Will we get to chat again soon?" Bass quickly asked.

I couldn't speak, but nodded yes before I disappeared. Bass put away his phone as JP sat down and said, "Dude, that was the tiniest bathroom I've ever seen!"

Bass smiled, but his stare lingered on the chair where I just sat. I wished I could have stayed longer.

CHAPTER THIRTY-THREE

After two amazing days in Venice, Bass and JP hopped on a flight back to London to stay for a day and a half before they had to fly back home to California.

The taxi driver that took them to their hotel sounded exactly like Paul McCartney. Bass thought he even looked like him, too. JP insisted he looked nothing like *Sir Paul* and that it was an insult to even insinuate as much.

Bass figured JP was acting sensitive because he was sick. He spent the previous night throwing up with some sort of food poisoning. JP clarified that his sickness had "moved south" but was feeling better. His pale white face said otherwise.

When they got to the hotel, Bass realized it was the same hotel they spent the first couple of nights in.

When they walked up to the front desk, it was even the same hotel agent who had attended to them on their first visit there. He had black hair with pinkish skin and a crooked nose, and he also happened to be one of the nicest people Bass had ever met.

Bass told him his last name and with a few clicks of the keyboard, the agent said, "Ah yes, here you are, sir. Welcome back gentlemen. It's good to have you back in London."

A COUNCIL OF ANGELS

"Thank you," Bass said.

He looked over to JP, who was sprawled across one of the chairs in the lobby. His face had turned from pale white to sickly green.

"Not feeling well, sir?" the agent inquired.

JP didn't speak. He just closed his eyes and shook his head no.

"Yeah, he probably ate a little too much gelato," Bass said.

"Understood sir."

With a few more clicks of the keyboard, the agent was done. He handed Bass two room keys and reminded him of the hotel's restaurant hours.

Bass thanked him and moved towards the elevator.

"Excuse me, sir," the agent called out. "One more thing."

Bass walked back up to the front desk. The agent pulled out a manila envelope and handed it to Bass and watched as he opened it.

Inside was Bass's wallet. He couldn't believe it. The cash was missing, but all of his cards were still there.

"A young woman returned the wallet here earlier today, sir," he said. "An American, actually." The clerk moved in closer and added, "She was quite a stunner." He gave Bass a wink.

Bass was shocked. "I don't understand," he started. "How did she know I was here?"

"You had your hotel room key in your wallet, sir," the agent said. "I checked your reservation and noticed you'd be passing back through. I'd say you had a travel angel with you, sir."

"I think you're right," Bass said, smiling. "Thank you very much. This just made my day."

Bass kicked JP's foot to get him off the chair, and they headed up to their room.

After opening the curtains to take in the view, Bass looked across the Thames to see Big Ben and the Palace of Westminster. It was a beautiful day, with only a few clouds passing by.

"Man, what a fantastic city!" Bass shouted.

JP was already lying facedown on the bed, moaning.

"Dude, that last Italian meal cursed me. Something is gurgling around in my guts."

"Well, I can't sit here. I gotta see this city one more time. I'm headed to the Natural History Museum. Wanna go?"

JP silently shook his head no. Bass got online quickly to check his bank accounts. They were untouched. He removed the hold on the accounts and with his money back, felt like a weight had been lifted.

"OK, so I'll be back soon. Do you need anything?"

JP shook his head no again.

Bass nodded to the front desk agent as he passed through the lobby and set out across the Westminster bridge. Just as he got to the other side, a lady with an old ragged coat stood in front of him, asking for some money.

"I don't have any cash. I'm sorry."

The woman got closer and groped his pockets.

"Come on, love, it's for the children. Just one quid."

"Whoa, excuse me!" he said. He stepped back, shocked at her boldness.

She kept coming at him, and he finally sidestepped her and hurried off the bridge. Once in a safe place, he turned around and watched her do the same thing to the next guy. He checked the map on his phone and headed off quickly towards the museum.

"Kind of like a bridge troll, huh?" a familiar voice said.

Bass jumped like a startled cat when he saw Rebekah walking next to him. She laughed. He chuckled, too. "Yeah, she was like a bridge troll." Bass sized up Rebekah's latest outfit. "So, you're some kind of British schoolgirl, I'm guessing?"

"Yes," Rebekah said starting in with a British accent, "it's a rather posh academy here in London."

She wore a red plaid skirt with a navy blue blazer that had some kind of golden crest embroidered on the lapel. A navy blue bow attempted to keep her red hair somewhat in place.

A COUNCIL OF ANGELS

"Are you visible right now?"

"Why? You don't want to be seen with a schoolgirl?"

Bass rolled his eyes. "I just want to know if I need to put my hands-free in or not."

"I'm telling you, Bassy, it's a big city. Nobody cares." Rebekah scurried to keep up with Bass's pace. She was almost skipping. "Where are you headed?"

"To the Natural History Museum."

"Why are you walking so fast?"

"I'm trying to avoid taking the tube and I've still got a long way to go."

"I see. What's at the museum?"

"Dinosaurs," Bass said. "I've always liked them and I know they have giant dinosaur skeletons there."

"You like dinosaurs?" Rebekah said with a tone that bordered on mockery. "How did I not already know that about you?"

"Well, it's not really something I tell everyone."

He saw her suppressing a giggle with her hands. She made a serious face, trying to hide the fact that she was laughing, and quickly changed the subject.

"Have you gotten any closer to finding your treasure?"

"Honestly, I'm not sure. I had a pretty cool experience in Rome. It's changed my point of view on a lot of things."

"I can tell…" She paused and then said, "Here's a fun question for you—have you thought about your dad at all?"

"What the…? Where did that come from?"

It was a tough subject for Bass. His dad died when he was five years old, leaving the family with very little. On some level, Bass resented him. He grew up without a dad and watched his mom work herself ragged to keep their little family going. Then again, it's part of what gave Bass his drive. He would never put his own family in that situation.

Rebekah asked, "Do you love your dad?"

"I barely even remember him!"

In reality, Bass only had two real memories of his dad. One was of his dad holding him after he got hurt while playing outside. He remembered watching his tears soak into his dad's shirt.

The other memory was rubbing his dad's bald head as he sat in a chair. The tiny hair stubs felt funny as Bass rubbed his hands back and forth.

Bass turned and followed the route on his phone, which took him right past the Spanish Embassy.

"How you feel about your parents can sometimes be complicated. No matter what though Bassy, you should love them. Period."

This was a sore subject for Bass, and it seemed like Rebekah knew it. She was more serious than usual. Bass walked faster, but Rebekah had no problem keeping up.

"If you had to name the single most obvious lesson your dad left you with, what would it be?"

Bass thought about it for a moment. He knew the answer, but wasn't sure if he wanted to admit it to Rebekah. He could hardly admit it to himself.

"Is this necessary Rebekah? I mean, the guy died when I was a kid. How was I supposed to learn anything from him?"

"Oh, I think you learned more than you're letting on, Bassy," she said.

He stopped walking. "Why do I need to say it out loud? Don't you already know? What's the point?"

"It's all part of the process."

He looked Rebekah in the eyes, and for a moment he saw her eyes flicker like tiny fires. It reminded him he was dealing with an angel. He sighed and sat down on the steps of a gray church. She sat next to him.

"He didn't leave anything," Bass said.

"What do you mean?"

"I mean, aside from literally leaving my mom with nothing, he didn't leave anything behind. Nothing that people remember him by. He was just some immigrant farmer guy named Joe that died from cancer."

"So why is that a lesson to you?"

"Because," Bass said, "it teaches me to make something of myself. You know my plan. I've already built and sold one business. Now I'm working on my next and it'll be 100 times bigger than my last business. Then I can make an even bigger difference in the world." He shot a glance at Rebekah. "I can do more of what I did in Rome. That was really cool."

"Ah, I see," she said. "You want to matter. You want to leave a legacy. I get it. It's important, but there are more ways to make a difference than just handing out money to people."

"What do you mean?"

"You made a difference in that family's life, no doubt. But it wasn't the money that did it. It was the connection they had with another human being. Somehow, a stranger from another country randomly gave them something they desperately needed that day. The real miracle for that family was your act of kindness. Their faith in humanity was restored and I can promise you it will have a ripple effect you can't even comprehend yet, Bassy."

Rebekah stood up and offered her hand to him. He reached for it and felt it. She lifted him up to his feet.

"I can feel your hand," he said. "I thought I couldn't touch you guys?"

"You couldn't. Past tense. But you felt Mary's hands, right?"

"Yes."

"It's because you're getting closer to finding your treasure. The closer you get, the more our worlds will merge."

"I still seriously don't even know what I'm supposed to be searching for."

"Oh Bassy, have you learned nothing? Keep serving. Love your way forward. Everything will open before you." She paused for a second, and Bass looked at her eyes. They glowed again.

"Soon your entire world will change. It's our job to get you ready. In fact, if I'm not mistaken, you only have 24 days left to work with us. Better pick up the pace, boy!"

Rebekah started skipping down the street, but she yelled back. "Have fun looking at a bunch of old dinosaur bones!" She giggled, jumped into the air, and faded from view.

Later that evening, Bass got back to the hotel and saw JP lying on the bed. He was watching TV, but looked like he hadn't moved at all.

"You OK?"

"Better. Just need to rest. I'm tired from too much walking to the bathroom."

"Gotcha."

"By the way, don't go in there. At least, not for a while."

"Gotcha."

Deciding to get some work done, Bass opened his laptop. His eyes widened as he noticed an email from Brittany. His fingers rested for just a moment on the keyboard before opening the email. He took a deep breath and clicked. It said:

Hey Bass

Having fun in Europe? Hope you're not mad at me. Real fast, I know of a buyer for your company. It's the real deal. We can chat more when you get home. Thought you'd like a heads-up.

XoXo
Brittany

CHAPTER THIRTY-FOUR

JP shook his head no adamantly, but Bass insisted.

"He does too. I'm not kidding!"

Bass thought their taxi driver looked like George Harrison. JP did not. They were on their way to the airport, leaving England behind.

"You think all British cab drivers look like one of The Beatles. It's ignorant. Shame on you."

"No, I don't think they *all* look like The Beatles. Only the last guy and this guy."

"They're the only two you've seen!"

"Sure, but it doesn't mean it's not true. It's just that these two guys look like Beatles."

"No, they don't. I should know. I'm literally named after two of them."

Bass looked back to the driver in the rearview mirror. He was an older guy and even had thick, dark eyebrows like George Harrison. He swore he could see the driver smiling to himself.

Can they hear us? he wondered.

The taxi pulled up to the curb at Heathrow Airport. The driver opened the door for them, and JP got out first. When Bass got out, he reached to give the driver a tip. He accepted the tip and said, "With every mistake we must surely be learning." He gave Bass a wink and got back in the taxi.

They walked down the path towards the airport entrance. Bass kept repeating the driver's words over and over. He knew he'd heard that phrase before.

Just before they got to the main doors, there was a group of about twenty people smoking. Bass's first instinct was to judge, but he caught himself. He looked at an older guy standing closest to the entrance. They locked eyes as they passed and Bass smiled and said, "Cool hat."

The guy took off his tweed cap, put it over his chest, and gave Bass an exaggerated nod and bow. Bass gave the man a small salute back as they entered the airport. After a quick look around, they made their way to the check-in counter.

"JP," Bass said, "what's this from—'with every mistake we must surely be learning'?"

"It's from 'While My Guitar Gently Weeps.' Everyone knows that," JP said. "Correction, all true Beatles experts like myself know that."

"Well, just so you know, that's literally what the taxi driver just said to me! I'm telling you, that guy was George Harrison."

"Dude, he's dead."

"Is he though? Is he?"

Five minutes later, they had their boarding passes, got through security, and meandered toward their gate.

"Hold on," JP said, "I gotta go to the bathroom, or 'loo' as the British say."

Bass posted in a spot a ways down from the bathroom doorway and observed everyone as they walked past. He practiced looking people in the eyes and smiling, and he even got a few smiles back.

"Finally," he said when JP came out.

A COUNCIL OF ANGELS

"Calm down, calm down," JP replied. "I'm still recovering from Venice, you know."

Out of nowhere, an older lady in a wheelchair scooted in front of them.

"You two look like very nice young men." She was American. "I need to get to my gate, but I'm not sure if I can make it there on my own. Would you mind giving me a push?"

JP looked at Bass with a devilish grin and put his arm around Bass's shoulders and said to the lady, "This guy is a surfer and has strong, muscular arms. He'll be happy to push you. Here, I'll take your suitcase."

"Thank you very much," the lady said, as Bass pushed her forward.

"Which gate are you heading to?" he asked.

"I don't remember but I am flying to Los Angeles."

"We are too," JP said. "How much you wanna bet we're on the same flight?"

He checked her ticket and said, "Hey whaddya know, we are on the same flight!"

As they got closer, the hallway became congested, full of people who looked like they'd been waiting for days to board their plane.

"This is it," JP said. "This is our gate."

"Oh, thank you very much for your help, gentlemen."

Bass walked in front of the lady and asked her name.

"My name is Susan," she said.

"Very nice to meet you, Susan," he said, shaking her hand. Then he pointed over to JP. "This guy here is John Paul. He was named after two of The Beatles."

"Oh my," the lady said. She leaned closer to JP and said, "John was always my favorite. Well, at least until that Yoko came along."

JP laughed, but Bass didn't get it.

What was a Yoko? he wondered.

"Thank you so much for your help."

Bass smiled. "No problem. Here, let me get you a little closer."

He wheeled Susan over to an area closest to the gate and looked back to JP, who already plopped down next to a column. All the seats were taken in the crowded airport. Bass walked over to his friend, who was busy untangling his cellphone charger.

JP shook his head and said, "I never thought I'd live to see the day when Mr. Sebastian Joseph Martinez would be pushing old ladies through the airport. I think this trip has changed you."

"Well, they say travel is like money or alcohol—it only amplifies what you already are. Maybe I'm a top-notch gentleman."

"Top-notch dork is more like it," JP said. "Still though, there's been a huge change in you. It's been fun to watch."

"Thanks man. I've had an absolute blast. And I haven't even really thought about work. So that's cool…I guess."

"I'm just glad you managed to find a way to help someone that doesn't involve giving them all of my money. Oh, and don't forget you owe me like a thousand dollars."

"I won't forget," Bass said.

The next hour flew past, and it was finally time to board the plane. Because of the crowds, Bass and JP accidentally got in the wrong line. An attendant who walked past checking tickets told them they needed to get in the other line, which was moving fast. They ducked under the ropes and ran up to the gate attendant.

As JP gave her his boarding pass, Bass felt someone looking at him. He glanced around quickly and saw a young woman staring directly at him. She was gorgeous. He desperately wanted to go talk to her.

"Your boarding pass, sir," the attendant said.

Bass looked down as the attendant scanned the pass. Once it beeped, he looked back at the girl. She smiled and then blew him a kiss. He couldn't believe it. She blew him a kiss! He felt a nudge of a handbag in his back as the person behind him shoved forward.

"Have a good flight, sir," the attendant said with a tone that really said, "move it or lose it, buddy!"

Bass took a few steps but managed a last minute pathetic wave before disappearing into the jetway. He caught up to JP, who was already stepping on the plane.

"Did you see that?"

"See what?"

"That girl!"

"Nope, sorry. No girl."

"She blew me a kiss!"

"Sure she did, buddy. Sure she did."

Bass dropped it, but kept thinking about the girl. Once they got in their seats, JP pulled out his floral print inflatable neck pillow while Bass opened his phone and popped in his hands-free to listen to some podcasts.

Before long, the plane lifted off the ground. In eleven hours, they would be back home in California. Bass tried to relax but kept thinking about the girl. He knew he'd seen her before. Then again, he'd seen so many faces in so many different places over the last two weeks—he just wasn't sure.

"I've got it!" he blurted out.

JP, who was half asleep already, mumbled, "What?"

"Dude," he nudged JP. "I know who that chick was! I saw her in the plaza—in that one Pickle Circus place."

"Piccadilly Circus," JP corrected.

"Whatever man. That was the girl!"

"Cool," JP said. He shifted his weight in his chair. "I'm happy for you, dude. Too bad she's in England and you're flying back to California."

"Yeah, but she's American. You can tell. And she was at the airport. If her plane was leaving by where ours left, doesn't it mean she's headed to the same part of the country as well?"

"Uh, I don't think that's how airports work," JP said.

"Still though, there's always hope, right?"

"What are you, like thirteen or something? We didn't even get a single girl's number and you're giddy about just *seeing* one?"

"You should have tried harder."

"Oh, I tried," JP said. "I like California girls better, anyway."

"Sure you do, buddy."

"Now, if you don't mind, I'd like to catch some Z's."

Bass corrected, "Don't you mean you'd like to catch some zeds?"

"Huh?"

"Never mind."

JP rolled over and closed his eyes.

Bass leaned back in his chair, feeling good. Tired, but good. Though he didn't know why, he was hopeful about his business. He was excited to get home and start working again.

Maybe that girl was part of it. He tried to memorize her face. He remembered the color of her hair. He was too far away to see her eyes. It was mostly the energy she had. She blew him a kiss. How cool was that? She didn't even know him, and he liked how bold she was. He loved it, in fact.

He closed his eyes and tried to sleep, but the image of the girl blowing him a kiss played over and over again in his mind.

CHAPTER THIRTY-FIVE

Skylar couldn't believe it. She'd heard stories about people getting bumped from their flights, but she didn't think it would ever happen to her.

"We're happy to arrange another flight home for you," the airline agent said. "Would you like me to do that now?"

"Naturally," she said. It came out with more attitude than she intended. "Thank you," she quickly added.

The agent nodded as he typed furiously at the keyboard. She turned and looked around at the busy airport. She was tired and wanted to sleep in her own bed in Huntington Beach. She missed her pillow. She'd been traveling by herself for over two weeks and while she loved every moment, was eager to get home.

"I've found you another nonstop flight that will actually arrive just an hour after your original flight."

Skylar nodded, but said nothing. The agent typed some more.

"If you like, for just $36 we can upgrade you to business class."

She turned back and looked at the agent.

"Really?"

"Yes. Should we use the same credit card you used to book your flight?"

"Yeah, that's fine," she answered. Her day was looking up. Sometimes seemingly bad things can lead to much better things. She'd never flown business class before. She wondered if it had leather seats and caviar, not that she'd ever eat fish eggs.

The agent handed Skylar a new boarding pass and pointed down the hall to the gate. She thanked him, grabbed her backpack and suitcase, and headed down the hall.

She noticed a couple of guys walking in through one of the main doors of the airport, clearly in the middle of a lively discussion. They were both handsome, especially the one with dark hair. She thought she recognized him somehow, like she'd seen him before. She watched them for a moment as they walked towards the check-in counter.

A loud grumble in her stomach reminded her she hadn't eaten in a while, so she made her way to a cafe and got a sausage roll. She sat down at a small table, opened her book, and took a bite. The bread was very flakey and half of it landed in her lap. She grabbed a napkin and brushed it off.

As she looked for a garbage can, she saw the same two guys again, speaking with a lady in a wheelchair. The blond one smiled and took the lady's suitcase while the dark handsome one started to push her. Skylar watched him as he walked down the corridor. She just knew she'd seen him before, but couldn't place it. She resolved that if she saw him again, she would talk to him.

Within a few minutes, Skylar finished her flakey sausage roll and washed it down with an orange juice. She read the last chapter of her book and swore. It occurred to her she didn't have any reading material for the plane. She looked at the book cover and contemplated reading it over again.

No, it wasn't that good, she thought.

She got up and headed back towards the bookstore she'd passed earlier. She picked up a sci-fi novel and two bags of

M&M's. She checked the bag to see if they were made in the UK. They were. She thought they tasted better than American M&M's.

"Here you are," the cashier said, handing Skylar the change. Without thinking, she dropped the coins into the charity cup next to the register.

"Cheers," the cashier said.

She nodded and took her time moseying down the terminal. She plowed into the book, looking up only to make sure she hadn't passed her gate. When she finally arrived, her shoulders slumped when she saw how many people were already there. She looked around the lounge but couldn't spot a single empty seat.

A guy with greasy black hair caught her eyes. He moved his stuff off of the chair next to him and smiled at her, pointing to the now empty chair.

Ugh, gross, she thought, but he'd already made the gesture, so she forced a smile and sat down.

"Thank you," she said. She put her carry-on suitcase under her chair and pulled her hoodie up closer around her head. She grabbed a lock of her hair and twisted it around in her fingers. She buried her face in the book, trying to close everything out, including the nostril-filling stench of the greasy guy's cologne.

A fast reader, she breezed through twelve chapters when she heard a boarding call. It was for the gate next to hers. She looked at the people in the line and realized the flight was also going to LA. There, at the front of the line, she saw the two guys again.

Then it hit her. She recognized the dark-haired guy. She first saw him in London and she was pretty sure he was the same guy she saw in Barcelona. It had to be! And now he was here in the airport, flying to Los Angeles.

It had to mean something, she thought.

She watched intently. The blond guy gave his boarding pass and walked away without waiting for his friend. The dark one caught her looking and stared back. She loved his face. It was kind. His eyes were dark but also bright somehow.

He looked away to give the attendant his boarding pass. She had to do something. What could she do? He was leaving *right now*. He glanced back towards her and, without thinking, she smiled and blew him a kiss. It wasn't something she'd normally do, but she liked this guy. He was handsome *and* he was kind.

The line moved forward, and the guy walked into the jetway. He gave a last-minute wave before disappearing. Skylar continued gazing towards the jetway, thinking of what else she could do.

"Maybe I'll see him in L.A.," she mumbled.

The greasy guy turned towards her. "What?"

"Oh, nothing. Sorry."

CHAPTER THIRTY-SIX

Bass sat in his office, staring absentmindedly at his laptop. I sat in an empty chair in the corner but, as usual, I wasn't visible. According to the calendar, only two days had passed since London, but Bass felt like it was only hours. Still in a daze, he'd only shuffled some papers and checked a few emails.

He wanted more sleep. He wanted to explore more of Europe. And he wanted to see that blond girl again.

He was sorting through his mail when someone knocked on the door. He looked to see Derrick, who was staring in through the glass. Bass waved him in.

Derrick sat down in the chair next to the door, where Bass usually kept his motorcycle helmet. He took a loud slurp of his coffee and asked, "How was Europe?"

"It was good," Bass said, nodding. "It was cool."

"Did you and your friend meet any ladies?"

Bass smiled and said, "No." He wasn't lying. He didn't *meet* any ladies. He *saw* one, but he didn't meet her.

"Anyway, I thought I'd let you know that your line went through. We were able to fast-track it after all."

"Wow, that's great. Thank you."

Derrick sat up in the chair and stared at Bass, sizing him up. He took a long slurp from his coffee, then looked at the old mug in his hands and said, "I've got to tell you something."

Bass perked up a little. Derrick's tone was different, humble almost.

"Here's the thing—I know you don't like me," he said. Bass shook his head no, but Derrick held his hand up to stop him. He brought his gaze back up to Bass and continued. "I know you call me Mr. Tight Pants Man or whatever. I don't really care. It works for me."

Bass's mind flooded with guilt, and he felt his cheeks getting red. Wishing it would stop, he put his hand over his face to hide it, pretending like he was listening intently.

Derrick took another slurp from his coffee. "I have a wonderful wife that loves me, two beautiful and healthy children and, in the end, that's all that really matters."

He took a deep breath and continued. "I'm sorry if you feel like I've ever tried to sabotage you. I really do want what's best for you and that means having a family. You shouldn't wait. I know you're busy trying to grow your business, but by then, it might be too late. I thought you and Brittany made a great team. But, it's not my business. Sorry."

Bass couldn't believe it. This was a total 180. He saw the guy in a completely different light. He thought instantly about Brittany. Maybe there was still hope.

Derrick stood up.

"Well," Bass started, "thank you for that. I mean, sorry if I've been a jerk, too. You're right though, I do need to get my priorities straight."

Derrick nodded as they shook hands, and then he turned and headed for the door.

"Hey, just one question," Bass said. "How'd you know I call you Mr. Tight Pants Man?"

A COUNCIL OF ANGELS

"I caught some punk in the warehouse calling me that. He said he got it from you."

"Sorry."

"What? It's true. Even my wife calls me that now."

He shrugged and walked out. Bass reached to shut the door and saw Haley in the hallway, straightening picture frames on the wall. He eyed her suspiciously.

"Were you just listening to all of that?"

"Huh, what?"

Bass squinted his eyes. "Yeah, right."

He sat back down at his desk and continued sorting through his mail. He saw a letter from a courthouse and wondered what it could be. As he opened it, I became visible and asked, "What's that?"

He jumped in his chair, and I couldn't help but laugh.

"Sorry," I said.

"Oh man, you scared me! Not sure if I'll ever get used to you guys randomly appearing like that."

"Sorry."

Bass looked at his office door, making sure it was closed, and then looked back at the letter. "It looks like I get to choose to go to some court thing for that guy that hit me."

"What will you do?"

Bass ran a hand through his hair, puffed his cheeks, and blew out loudly. "Oh man, I don't know."

"Are you upset with him still?"

Bass looked down at his leg. The scabs were already gone, leaving only some light scars. He thought about it for a moment and said, "No, I don't think so. Honestly, I'm kind of concerned about him. Don't drunk drivers go to jail?"

"I have no idea about that stuff," I replied.

"Are there any legal angels I can speak with?"

"You mean like lawyer angels?"

"Yeah."

"No. I'm pretty sure that would be a contradiction in terms. Besides, I think the other guys get the lawyers."

CHAPTER THIRTY-SEVEN

A day after meeting with Derrick, Bass got a text from Jen. It said, "Bass, meant to meet with you today. Sorry. Finalizing the plans of the sale."

Bass replied immediately, "You mean your business?"

"Yes. In part, it relates to yours as well because the buyer will acquire all of my business interests, including my share in your business."

"OK…"

"It's good. Don't worry. You'll be fine."

"OK."

"I think the new buyer will meet with you sometime soon. Gotta go!"

"OK."

CHAPTER THIRTY-EIGHT

"We've been home for what, four days already? And this is the first time we get tacos? What's wrong with us?"

JP was talking with a mouth full of food, as usual. A tiny chunk of guacamole shot out of his mouth, landing on his hand, but he didn't notice or seem to mind.

He and Bass were working through an entire bag of takeout from Pancho's. They sat outside on Bass's patio with their feet kicked up on the fence so they could look towards the beach. The sun was setting, casting oranges and reds into the sky. A light breeze brought in the sweet smell of the ocean.

"Dude, I forgot how much I missed Mexican food. It makes me happy," Bass said. "It probably makes my ancestors happy that I love it so much."

"Whoa, look at you! Finally, embracing your Mexican heritage," JP said, pouring a bunch of hot sauce onto his taco. "Too bad you're a whoosy boy when it comes to jalapeños."

"Well, I am also half-German too, you know."

"Whatever, you're a mutt like the rest of us..." JP got distracted by a gorgeous, dark-haired woman walking past on

180

A COUNCIL OF ANGELS

the sidewalk. She stopped in front of the patio and Bass practically choked on his taco when he realized it was Brittany.

She was wearing a gray skirt with a red blouse, the top few buttons undone. Her red heels gave her a few more inches than normal, and her dark, wavy hair hung down past her shoulders. She had a tablet in her hand.

"Hi Bass. Can I come in?"

"Uh, yeah, sure."

She walked through the patio gate and leaned down to give Bass a light hug and a kiss on the cheek.

She smells amazing, he thought.

"We're just eating some tacos. Would you like one?"

"No, thank you," she said.

JP quickly scanned her up and down. "Sup?"

"Hey JP. How's it going?"

"Well, I've got a mouthful of tacos, it's shaping up to be a beautiful sunset, and I'm chillin' with my best friend. Life's pretty good."

Brittany smiled and sat down next to JP in a chair facing Bass.

"Your hair looks good," JP said.

"Thanks," she replied. "It better for $350."

"What's up?" Bass asked, with an edge to his voice.

Honestly, he had no idea why she was there. She looked fantastic, but something didn't feel right. JP shoved another taco into his mouth.

"How was Europe?"

"It was good. We had a lot of fun..." Bass caught himself starting to blab but cut himself off. He wanted to know why she was there and why she was all dressed up. "What brings you by?"

"I just left a meeting with Jen," she started.

Bass's mind jumped into overdrive. *Why would she be in a meeting with Jen?*

181

"I'm not sure what she's told you but long story short, my family has been in talks with her to acquire her business."

Inside, Bass felt like he just got hit by a tsunami. It required every ounce of his energy to stay still.

What would this mean to my company? What would this mean to me? Would I see Brittany every day?

As the thoughts flooded his brain, he wore his best poker face, trying to not even blink. He raised his eyebrows and said, "Wow. That's cool."

"Yes. We're also looking at buying her shares of your company. As you know, it's a 30% stake. She's been content to sit in the background all these years, but we would like to take a more active role."

"What do you mean?" Bass sat up. Something about her tone made him feel like his entire empire, his life plans, were suddenly slipping through his fingers. He glanced at JP, whose eyes were wide. He stopped eating and sat back in his chair.

"Well, Bass, we think we can take your company to the next level. You've done an amazing job and you should be proud. But now, we can make it an international brand."

"Why do you want to own a surf line? It's not your target market or what you guys are even good at."

"We'd like to add it to the portfolio."

Bass looked up to the sky, trying to take it all in. He needed more info. "What will happen then?"

"Well, there are a few options. You can either let us come on as your new partner with a more active role, or you can buy back the 30% share..." Brittany paused for a second. "Or you can sell the entire company to us."

Bass couldn't believe his ears. This was really happening, but he never expected it to happen like this. He'd worked hard for this, but it didn't feel right. Something was off.

"What's the price you're looking at?"

A COUNCIL OF ANGELS

"We need to take a hard look at the books but I've been authorized to offer up to $1.1 million."

It was a shock, an insult. It was much lower than what Bass was expecting. He anticipated selling for at least $5 million, or more, when the time came.

"Bass," she said, "I know what you're thinking, but trust me, your company isn't as valuable as you think it is."

He didn't reply. It was a dig. It was also negotiations. He remained quiet. It felt like she was intentionally snubbing him with the price. Out of the corner of his eye, Bass caught JP looking at him and watched as he, ever so slightly, shook his head no.

"Umm, I need to use the loo," JP said as he stood up and walked into the house.

Brittany waited for him to close the door, and then she sat forward and put a hand on Bass's leg. He looked down, noticing her newly manicured nails with glossy red polish.

"Bass, this could be the big time for you. If you don't sell and stick with it, this means crazy growth. You know the resources my family has. That, together with you and I running the show, there's no stopping us. We've already got some big names lined up to endorse your brand. We just need to know what you want to do."

Bass sat back in his chair and adjusted his leg, letting Brittany's hand drop. Something in his gut was telling him it was wrong.

"What do you mean by running the show *together*?"

Brittany tilted her head and said, "I've seen your dedication, and I know you can make this big. I think we'd be a great team. I think we could do it professionally." She leaned in closer and put her hand back on his leg. "And, I think we could go for it as a couple as well."

"A couple? You and me? Yeah, well, I'm confused. When I felt something, and actually opened up to you, I pretty much got dropped the next day. That's changed now?"

"Yes, you seem different, like you've changed. Maybe taking a break was just what we needed." She leaned in even closer. "Bass, think carefully about what's being offered here."

JP opened the door, headed back out to the patio, and his eyes zeroed in on Brittany's hand on Bass's leg. She pulled back as he got closer. He plopped down and reached in the bag for another taco.

Bass's head was spinning. "I need to think," he said.

Brittany nodded and stood up. "I totally get it."

Bass got up as well and walked her to the patio gate. She leaned in and kissed him on the cheek.

"I'll be in touch," she said. She took a step backward and added, "Bass, we're moving quickly on this. You'll need to decide fast. Within two weeks at the latest."

Bass nodded and closed the gate behind her. He turned back to look at his best friend.

"Another taco?" JP asked, but he already knew the answer. "Why don't I just eat the last one."

CHAPTER THIRTY-NINE

The morning after Brittany came by, Bass woke up before dawn. He wasn't going surfing, he just couldn't sleep. He rolled out of bed, took a shower, and then opened his laptop to check emails.

The first message was from Kathy. He groaned out loud, suddenly feeling guilty for not even calling her since he got back. He made a mental note to do so. He clicked on her email and it read:

Hi Bass,

I want to hear all about Europe! Maybe I can try to make it down sometime soon. I've been picking up some extra shifts, but I want to try to see you. If not, maybe you can come up here? I promise not to ambush you with more family history!

Actually, there is something I've been meaning to tell you. I wanted to tell you all of this in person because it's very important. I just don't know if I would be able to get it out without falling apart. As it is, I've already written and rewritten this four times. I don't know why, but I also feel an overwhelming need to make sure you know what I'm about to share.

OK, here goes...

First, regardless of what happens with your business, I hope you'll meet someone soon. Don't wait Bass. Don't worry, I'm not pressuring you for grandkids. I just want you to be happy. I know the right woman is out there. You'll recognize her when the time is right. It will be the most important decision you'll ever make.

Now, I've had this pressing feeling that I need to tell you what happened with your father. I'm not sure why, but I need to tell you. I know we've both always shied away from this subject, but I need to share this. I need to share the truth.

When you were young, about four years old, your father got really sick. He came home early from work one day coughing up blood. We took him to the hospital, and they ran some tests. Long story short, we found out he had lung cancer. It was a huge surprise to us because he never smoked and was generally very healthy.

I'm pretty sure it was a result of his exposure to the pesticides they used on the farm where he worked. It was already pretty advanced, and he became very sick. They tried chemo and that kept it at bay for a year or so, but his health was getting worse.

Just after you turned five years old, I wanted him to be able to get outside for once and spend some time together as a family. We took a trip up to the mountains. It was October, and we had

A COUNCIL OF ANGELS

the campground to ourselves. You were playing on a dock by the lake with your dad when you fell in.

Bass, this is so hard to write. But, I feel really strongly that I should share this with you.

You fell in and the water was deep. You were still so small and you didn't know how to swim yet. Without even thinking, your father jumped in immediately to get you. He managed to push you up onto the dock, but the cold water weakened him. He fought hard and finally got out of the water, but it took a lot out of him.

He carried you back to camp, and you two were both soaking wet when you got back. His lips were blue, and he was shivering uncontrollably. He just didn't have any muscle or fat left. He also didn't have any immunity. As a result, he developed pneumonia.

He fought hard, but he passed away a week later. The final day in the hospital, he kept calling your name. I didn't want you to see him in the hospital like that. I'm so sorry Bass. Not a day goes by where I wish he could have said goodbye to you. I just didn't want your last image of him to be that of being hooked up to tubes. I realize this was so incredibly selfish of me. I hope you'll forgive me. I am so, so sorry.

Bass, I never told you any of this, especially when you were a kid, because I never wanted you to feel like you were to blame. It was nobody's fault. Do you understand? It was nobody's fault. Your dad did what any parent would do. In fact, it's what we're supposed to do as parents.

I know you've never been able to really deal with this. I hope this information helps though.

I want you to know that your father was an admirable man. No, he didn't leave much behind for us, but that's OK. We managed. I think you and I made a wonderful team.

I loved your father. He never won any accolades. He wasn't famous. He never made a lot of money. But everyone that knew him loved him. He made people feel good wherever he was. He worked hard. I think you get your work ethic from him. He served people. His focus was always on others. He was always the first to collect everyone's dishes after a meal or to cheer someone up or to help with a chore.

When he passed away, I was devastated. I wanted to save you from that. You were only five years old, so I buried it deep down. I'm so sorry. As I write this, it almost seems more of a confession than anything else. I am sorry I wasn't there for you more. You're so independent and I've always tried to respect that. I wish we could spend more time together now, though.

Bass, I love your father. Somehow, in a way I can't describe, I know he goes on. I also see him every time I look at you. I think he'd be so proud of the man you've become. I have a strong hope that we will all be together again.

If you're upset with me, I completely understand. If you need time, I understand that too.

I love you Bass. I love you so, so much. I'm so proud of you.

Love you,
Mom

Bass closed his laptop. He stood up, but his legs buckled and he dropped to the floor. He crawled to the couch, buried his face into the cushions, and lost control of his emotions.

CHAPTER FORTY

I have to say that this part of Bass's journey was especially hard for me. I wish I could have hugged the boy. I wish I could have shared some words of encouragement.

But at this point, it wasn't yet part of my assignment. When I did get to appear, my job was to help him think and find his own solutions. But like I said, it was hard.

In fact, Bass lost an entire day after reading Kathy's email. He stayed at home. He didn't eat. He didn't drink. He spent the better part of the day simply laying on the floor in his bedroom.

It was so much to process. At first, he was upset with his mother, but as the day progressed, he didn't blame her. He reasoned that he would have done the same thing.

The more he thought about her, the more he felt so sorry for her—to think of the emotions she must have dealt with over the years.

Before Bass even realized it, it was dark out. He got ready for bed and crawled under his covers. His thoughts shifted to his father. Before falling asleep, a single thought repeated itself over and over in his mind.

My father gave his life to save mine.

A COUNCIL OF ANGELS

The next day, Bass woke up again before dawn. He sat up in his bed, wide awake. Almost trancelike, he walked downstairs, grabbed his surfboard, and headed for the beach. He paddled out and caught every single wave he tried for. Somehow, each new wave increased his energy, bringing him back to life.

After a couple of hours, he made his way back to shore. As he stared back out at the sets coming in, he realized his life was different. His entire worldview was changing. His own father was no longer some poor immigrant farmer who left him with nothing. His father was a hero. Bass felt an upwelling of love for him as well as an increased desire to learn more about him.

He suddenly remembered his mom and ran home to call her. When he got home and grabbed his phone, he saw a text from Brittany.

"We need a decision. I, need a decision."

Bass ignored it. He called his mom but got her voicemail. He quickly texted her.

"Mom, thank you for your email. It changed my life. No joke. Thank you. I love you. Let's meet up soon."

Bass wrote a follow-up message. "Yes, even if that means I have to drive up to old people town." He added a smiley face and sent the text.

Bass went out to the garage and pulled off his wetsuit. He put his surfboard back on the rack alongside with his other boards. He looked around his garage. There, where he always kept it, was his mountain bike. He hardly used it, but today seemed like a good day to ride. Work could wait. He needed to figure out what that even meant, anyway.

After a quick change, Bass set off down PCH, headed south towards Newport Beach. He rode fast and before he knew it, he turned right onto the bridge to Balboa Island. He rode casually and made it to the northernmost point of the island. He circled back and rode down Emerald avenue. He got off his bike and walked out onto the public pier.

He walked down the pier to the floating dock, took his shoes off, and put his feet in the water.

It was finally my time to engage a bit more with the boy, and I felt myself appear. I sat down next to Bass and put my feet in the water as well. He looked at me but didn't act surprised this time.

"Hey," he said.

"Hey, Bass. How are you?"

"Good," he replied. "But why aren't your feet making any ripples in the water?"

To be honest, I didn't know. I just shrugged and for some reason, that made Bass laugh. It was good to see. He needed it.

"What are you going to do?" I asked.

"What do you mean?"

"I saw what happened with Brittany. What are your thoughts on the whole thing?"

"Honestly, I don't know." Bass looked at his feet in the water. He kicked back and forth. "Something about it doesn't feel right, though."

"Do you feel you have enough information to make a decision?"

"Yeah, that's all clear. I looked over the official paperwork, but I just don't know what to do. It used to be all so straightforward. I always wanted to sell this business but now, it doesn't feel right. At least, not like this."

We looked up to see a family on paddle boards moving past us. The mom was in front, followed by four boys with the dad in the back. Each of the four boys had their own paddle board, except for the youngest, who was on his dad's board. The boy dragged two fingers through the water like miniature waterskis.

Bass looked at me and said, "Am I getting closer? I mean, am I getting closer to my treasure? I used to think it was selling my business, but now I'm not so sure. I don't know what it is, actually."

I searched for the right answer to give him. I wish I could

have tapped into Mary's wisdom or Jacob's directness. I answered honestly, based on the info I'd been given so far.

"Yes, Bass," I said. "I think you are."

"I still don't even know what it means. I've just been going kind of blind here."

"Well, that's part of having faith. Sometimes you can't see the whole trail, just the steps right in front of you," I said. "But you're on the right path. That much I *do* know."

"Can you tell me what to do about my business? And what should I do about Brittany? I mean, basically at the core of it all, she's offering two things—money and love. With her family's resources, I could grow it into the company I've always wanted. And then with Brittany, I mean, wow, you know what she looks like, right?"

"Yeah, I know what she looks like." I turned to look at Bass and asked, "Then why the hesitation?"

"Yeah, that's a good question," Bass said. "I don't know." He looked down at the dock. A fisherman left some salmon eggs there. Bass picked one up and threw it in the water. We watched as some tiny fish darted around the egg as it sank to the bottom. Then a dark shape moved in and in a flash the egg was gone.

"I suppose it just doesn't feel right," he said.

"So you're making the decision to say no?"

"I suppose so. It's crazy. If any other guy in the world knew what I was saying no to, he would think I'm nuts."

"Then you're making a faith-based decision."

"A faith-based decision?"

"Yes. When anyone makes a decision without knowing all the information or consequences, it comes from one of two places, faith or fear."

Bass nodded his head, processing what I was saying. I continued, "Right now, if you were to make a fear-based decision, you would go for the sure thing—the money, the girl. But it doesn't feel right to you. And something deep down is telling you there might just be something better out there. That's faith, the hope of something better."

"You're an angel, so you work for God, right? Can't you just ask him and have him tell me what I should do?"

"Yeah, I could have him tell you what to do. But," I said, "do you think you'd really listen?"

Bass chuckled. "I don't know," he replied. "Maybe I would now? What do you think? What do I do instead?"

"You've got to trust your feelings and decide. If it's the right decision, you'll feel it's right. If it's wrong, you'll feel confused and then you'll know. Remember what Rebekah taught you in Paris? What did she say again? You either live in fear or you live in love. That's sound advice."

Bass nodded his head in agreement. Just then, his phone buzzed. He looked at it, ignored it, but pulled his feet out of the water. He stood up, put his shoes back on, and said, "I have another question."

"Shoot," I said.

"Do you know if my dad is in heaven?"

His question came out of nowhere, and I wasn't ready to answer it. I tried to talk, but only managed to squeak out an answer.

"Yes, he's in heaven."

Bass was quiet for a minute and then asked, "Can you describe what heaven is like?"

"No, not really."

"Is it because you're not allowed to or something?"

"I'm allowed. It's just really hard to describe."

"Can you compare it to something? Something here on earth? Something my human brain could understand?"

It was a fantastic question. I looked out to the harbor and watched the sunlight sparkle on the water's surface.

"The closest thing I can think of would be lights," I said.

A COUNCIL OF ANGELS

"Lights?" Bass replied. "What kind of lights? Like a flashlight? Christmas lights? Stadium lights?"

"No, no, not like that. Just an all-enveloping light that hits you on every level."

Bass started walking up the pier to get his bike.

"I don't get it," he said.

"You'll know it when you see it."

"What do you mean? Can I see it here? Don't I have to die or something?"

"Nope. You can see little pieces of heaven right here on earth." I paused to think if what I wanted to say was OK. I think it was. "If you stay on this path, you're going to see a little piece of heaven very soon."

Bass turned back to me with a look of hope on his face.

"Really?"

"Yes," and then I desperately hoped what I said was OK.

CHAPTER FORTY-ONE

After getting home from his bike ride, Bass texted Brittany.

"I'm holding on to my company. I'm going to buy back the 30%."

He got a message almost immediately.

"How are you going to do that? Wait. Doesn't matter. OK. If that's what you want. We'll start the process."

Another message came almost immediately.

"What about us?"

Bass replied, "Sorry, but no."

There was no reply.

He put the phone down. He didn't know why or how yet, but everything felt right. He had no clue how he was going to come up with that much money, but it didn't seem to bother him.

Strangely, he was feeling good. Life was looking up.

PART III

TO ACT

May 14, 6:00 a.m.

Greetings Team,

It's been a couple of days since any of us have made contact, but I believe things are on schedule.

However, if I'm not mistaken, tomorrow is the day. Of course, you can imagine the whirlwind of emotions I'm already going through.

Please, I'll need your help with Bass. He's come so far. I really hope he can make it through this. He's going to feel so alone. I know it's going to be hard to watch.

Again, I ask for your help for the both of us. Please.

Warm Regards,
Michael

CHAPTER FORTY-TWO

After speaking with me at the pier, Bass made several changes. He first spoke with Jen, who was very supportive of his decision.

She still had to remain on for six months as part of the transition, but then she was free. She was going to refocus her life to help young girls in Central American countries get access to quality education. Bass admired her and realized that he was slightly envious of her total devotion to the cause.

After telling Brittany he was going on his own, Bass was in his office, thinking about his options. Haley came by and knocked on the door.

"Come in," Bass said.

Haley sat down and said, "I heard what you're going to do. It's so cool! I'm happy for you."

"Thank you," Bass said. "What about you? Will you continue on to work with Brittany's company?"

"I think so. They weren't clear about my position but I know the rest of the senior management is part of the package, even Mr. Tight Pants Man."

"You don't sound too excited."

"To be honest, it's not what I thought I'd be doing with my life," she said. "Don't get me wrong—I like this job, but I want to have more time with my daughter. Before I know it, she'll be off to college. I feel like I spend half my life just commuting."

Bass's phone buzzed on his desk. He looked at the number and didn't recognize it.

"You're not going to answer that?"

Bass shrugged.

Haley started to say something but stopped.

"What?"

"I was wondering how you're going to come up with the money to buy back Jen's share of the business? And what about your setup here? Will you be able to continue to use the facilities to fill your orders?"

Bass leaned back in his chair and sighed. "I'm not sure. I guess it really depends how much they value my business. I was thinking of going on my own but looking at the numbers, even if I lease everything, it's gonna sting."

Bass's phone buzzed again. It was the same number.

"I better take this," he said.

Haley waved and left his office.

"Hello?"

"Can I speak with Sebastian Martinez?"

"That's me."

"Mr. Martinez, my name is Dr. Wendy Jones from the Community Hospital near Monterey."

Bass immediately tried to remember if that's where his mom worked. He wished he'd paid more attention.

"Sebastian," she said, her tone slow and deliberate, "I'm sorry to have to tell you this over the phone but your mother, Katherine Martinez, passed away today..."

Bass stopped listening. It couldn't be. He stared down at his desk, but his vision blurred. The lights in his office seemed to darken, and he felt like the ceiling pushed down on him.

A COUNCIL OF ANGELS

The voice continued. "They brought her in after fainting in a grocery store near here. She suffered a stroke. From what I could tell, it was due to an atrial fibrillation. There was an unusual amount of blood that had pooled in her heart, which I believe led to a clot. The clot traveled to her brain and caused the stroke."

The voice stopped. Bass couldn't speak. His mouth felt like it had been wired shut. He was numb.

It had to be a dream, he thought.

"Sebastian? Are you there?"

He spoke, but no sound came. He cleared his throat. "Yes, I'm here."

"Do you understand what I just shared with you?"

"Yes."

"We tried our best, but we weren't able to resuscitate her after she arrived. I'm very sorry." The doctor waited on the line. "Sebastian?"

"Yes," Bass whispered.

"I'm very sorry for this. I have to ask this because you're her only family. We'll need you to come here and make the arrangements. Is this number your cell phone?"

"Yes," Bass whispered again.

"I'll text you with some information and numbers. Do you have any questions for me?"

"Yes," Bass struggled to get the words out. "My mom is...dead?"

There was a pause and then the doctor said, "Yes. I'm so sorry." She added, "I will also send you more information for help in dealing with this. Would you like that?"

"Yes."

"I'll send that to you now. Again, I'm so sorry."

"OK."

"Goodbye," she said.

"Bye."

He put his phone down on his desk and stared at it. After a

203

moment, he closed his laptop, grabbed his stuff, and left the office. Somehow, he made it to the car but suddenly found himself with his head on the steering wheel, sobbing from the deepest parts of his soul.

CHAPTER FORTY-THREE

"Can I get you anything, man?"

"No, I'm good. Thank you though, JP."

"Cool. If you don't mind, I'm going back for another round of cookies."

It was only two days after Bass got the phone call letting him know his mother passed away. He sat on a chair outside the chapel in the funeral home in Monterey. The services were now over. He'd chosen not to speak. He still felt numb and in no condition for any public speaking.

Several of Kathy's coworkers and neighbors passed by and offered him their condolences, all saying nice things about her. He spoke with them, but it was like he was inside his own head, merely watching a movie play out in front of him.

After a while, the funeral home director approached Bass and said, "Mr. Martinez, this is the urn that contains your mother's ashes. As you can see, it's exquisite."

"Thank you," he said, but didn't reach up to take the urn.

The director said a few more things and seemed to be proud of how quickly they were able to arrange the services. When Bass didn't reply, he changed gears and began sharing the five stages

205

of grief. JP came back with a plate of cookies, but quickly read Bass's expression. JP intervened and thanked the director, took the urn from him, and escorted Bass out of the funeral home.

Later that afternoon, JP drove Bass over to Kathy's house. After pulling up, the couple that owned the main home came outside and expressed their condolences, and shared a few nice sentiments about Kathy. Bass simply smiled and moved towards the small home where his mother used to live, while JP stayed behind to talk with the couple.

Bass placed the urn on the kitchen counter. It seemed almost wrong, but he wasn't sure what else to do. He moved to her bedroom and sat on her bed. He looked around her room at all of her things. Her hospital ID badge hung from the mirror, her golf clubs were in the corner, and there was a pile of change with some golf tees on her dresser.

He looked at her nightstand. Next to her lamp was a picture of him. It was a photo Kathy took at his high school graduation. JP was pretending to eat his graduation cap, and Bass was crossing his eyes with his tongue sticking out.

Next to the photo was Bass's business card from his landscaping business. Underneath was another business card from his apparel company.

Next to his business cards was a note. It was old—the edges yellowed from time. He opened it carefully and read it.

My Beautiful Katherine, My Light

I've never met a woman like you before in my life. When I first saw you, you were brighter than the noonday sun. You still radiate pure, positive energy.

You make me feel whole. I still cannot believe that you said yes to marrying me.

I will work hard every day of my life to make you happy. We will raise a big family and grow old together.

You are my love. You are my light. You are my sweetest friend. I am forever yours.

Joe

Bass closed the letter and put it back on the dresser. His hands tightened into fists and he yelled at the sky.

"Why God?" he cried. A groan came from deep within him and turned into a pathetic whimper. He fell to the ground, his knees hitting first. He slammed the floor with his fists.

"Why? I don't understand," he whispered. "They were supposed to grow old together. Why even let them meet? Why even let them fall in love? Why let them have me? Just so I could be born, lose my father, and then lose my mother?"

His chest tightened, and he couldn't breathe. He buried his face in the carpet and cried until he started coughing. He got up to wash his face in the bathroom. He couldn't even look at himself in the mirror. He did his best to breathe normally, but the urge to cry was trying to fight its way out.

He sat back down on the floor, looked at the letter again, and then hung his head and prayed.

"Please God, I don't understand. Just when I thought I was beginning to make things better with my mom." He paused to breathe again, trying to remain calm. "And now you take her? I don't get it."

Without looking up, Bass felt someone else enter the room and a moment later, he was being lifted by two powerful hands under his arms. It was Jacob. He placed Bass on the bed and sat down next to him. Bass wiped his eyes, suddenly feeling embarrassed. Mary was there too, and Rebekah was leaning against the bedroom door. They all wore white clothing, even Rebekah.

Bass sniffed, dried his eyes with his shirt, and tried to compose himself. They all smiled and waited for him to speak.

He couldn't bring himself to make eye contact with any of them. "Sorry, but I'm not really in the mood for a lecture."

"We're not here to lecture you, Sebastian," Mary said. Without another word, she sat next to him on the bed and gave him a hug. He could actually feel her arms around him. He suddenly felt warm, and his muscles seemed to go slack as he fell into Mary's embrace. He felt the beating of his own heart, and a sense of love and completeness raced through his soul.

Two seconds later, Rebekah walked over and wrapped her arms around them. Somehow, the love intensified, and Bass surrendered to the feeling.

Then Jacob leaned in and hugged all of them, and the feeling almost overcame him. They stayed that way for a while. All the previous tension in his body melted away, and he breathed deeply and calmly.

One by one, the angels slowly let go of Bass.

"For the record, that's called 'love' and it's my specialty," Rebekah said.

She was suddenly sitting crisscrossed on top of the dresser, where she held Kathy's phone, but didn't look up from the screen. Jacob gave her a high five as he walked past and took up a position in the doorway, looking between both rooms with his arms folded. Mary remained on the bed next to Bass.

He looked around and said, "Thank you, guys."

The angels smiled, and Bass realized Mary was right. They weren't there to lecture him—they were simply there.

After a moment, Bass broke the silence. "I've got to admit, and I hope I don't offend you guys or whatever, but I'm still upset with God. It doesn't seem fair."

Mary nodded, wanting him to continue.

"I mean, I just found out about my dad. He was cool! He literally saved my life. And he gave his life..." Bass trailed off as his throat tightened. He took a deep breath and continued. "And now, just when I was about to try to really connect with my mom, she's taken. And it really hurts to know I wasn't there for her. I didn't get to be with her when she passed."

Jacob perked up and said, "Come on, sport. Based on what you know of her, do you think she would have wanted you there to see her die? She wants you to dwell on the happy, not the sad."

"Not to be rude but, how can you say that? You didn't even know her."

"Oh, we know her," Jacob said.

Bass narrowed his eyes. "Huh?"

Mary gave Jacob a look. He shot her a look back as if to say, "What?"

"Sebastian," Mary said, "this is what every parent wishes—to see their children grow up to be happy and successful with families of their own."

"Yeah, that's the last of my worries now."

Mary looked over to Rebekah, who gave her a wink.

"Bassy, we'll be in touch," she said. "But maybe you should take a look at this."

Rebekah handed Bass Kathy's phone. He stared at the screen in shock. He looked up, but Rebekah, along with Mary and Jacob, had already vanished. His eyes went back to the cell phone. He saw the last text he sent to his mom. It was right after surfing when he thanked her for sending the email. That seemed like an eternity ago.

He saw that she typed a response. Cleary, she never hit the send button. It read:

Thank you so much for that, Bass. It means so much to me. Don't worry about coming to my old people town. I'll come down to your young people town, if you don't mind. I want to see your photos from Europe, anyway. I'll call you soon. I love you. You mean the world to me.

Bass read the message three times. He could no longer cry. He felt dried up.

He stood, walked towards the mirror and stared at his reflection. He looked himself in the eyes and made a resolution then and there to live up to what his mother thought of him. He would be the man she raised him to be.

CHAPTER FORTY-FOUR

Bass and JP stayed the night in a hotel. Something felt wrong about sleeping in Kathy's home.

The next morning, they got up early to get started with the day. They rented a moving truck and bought a bunch of boxes. Bass decided to haul all of Kathy's stuff down to his house where he could sort through it later. The couple who owned the home said there was no rush, but he wanted to get it over with.

They started in the front room. JP went over to the computer, sat down in the chair, moved the mouse, and the screen turned on. The screen saver was of a young Kathy smiling and holding a baby with dark hair. Bass came over and stared at the photo. He'd never seen it before.

JP laughed. "Dude, is that baby Bass?"

As he glanced at the look on Bass's face, JP knew it wasn't a time to joke. He realized everything was still very raw for Bass.

"Umm, you know what we're missing right now?"

Bass didn't respond.

"We can't have a moving day without donuts!" JP said. "I'm gonna get some. I'll be right back."

Bass nodded his head, and JP stood up and dashed out the

front door. Bass sat down on his mom's computer chair and stared at the picture. Kathy was so happy in that photo.

He turned in the chair and hit his leg against one of the legs of the desk, which sent a stack of folders crashing to the floor. He reached down to pick them up and noticed each folder had a name labeled on it.

The first one said, Rebekah & Diego. He opened the file and saw a family tree diagram. Behind it were photos, photocopies, and a yellow legal pad full of Kathy's handwritten notes. The top page said, "Rebekah and Diego. Married 64 years. Happy marriage. See box of love letters."

Bass pulled out a black-and-white photo of a couple. The woman had big, curly hair.

"It can't be," Bass said out loud.

He reached for another folder that said Martinez Line. Inside, Bass saw more notes his mother had written. Attached to the file was a photo of a young woman with thick black hair down past her shoulders. Her face was solemn, yet peaceful. She held a small baby boy in her lap.

The next file he picked up said Heidelberg Line. He flipped through the notes and found lists and lists of names. A picture dropped out of the file and as he reached down, he could tell it was extremely old. He flipped the photo in his hand and saw a tall, bald man with piercing eyes. A yellow sticky note was attached where Kathy scribbled a name: Jakob Schneider.

"It can't be," Bass said again.

Bass looked through the rest of the box and found more folders with names. It was a treasure chest of knowledge about his ancestors.

Then he noticed another box. The lid said, "All notes on Joe." Bass's chest got tight, but he took a breath and opened the box. On top of the stack was a photo of a young Kathy and her husband, Joe. He had thick, dark hair. Bass was shocked at how much his dad looked like him. His eyes were clear, his face bright.

A COUNCIL OF ANGELS

He opened a folder that had hospital bills and papers. He flipped through and read words like, 'prognosis' and 'extremely advanced' and 'stage 4'. He reached for a note with his mother's handwriting.

As he picked up the note, he suddenly stopped moving. He sensed me standing behind him. I put my hand on his shoulder. He moved as he could actually feel my hand. He began to shake. He reached for my hand and touched it, squeezing my hand in his. It was electric as his whole body seemed to fill with a glowing energy.

In a single, overwhelming instant, he realized who I was. He didn't look up, but opened his mouth to speak.

"Dad?" He struggled to say the words. "Is it really you?"

I was overcome. I could barely speak. I breathed deeply.

"Yes, son. It's me," I whispered.

Large tears flooded Bass's eyes and spilled over onto his cheeks. He stood and turned to look at me. He let out a small gasp as he really saw me for the first time. I pulled him in and we embraced. He felt so tall. He was trembling. I pulled him in tighter.

"I can't believe it," he said. "This whole time you have been right in front of me and I never knew. How?"

I smiled. It's all I could do. I released him and motioned to the sofa. I moved a vase full of flowers from the funeral to make room. We sat on the sofa for a small eternity, not moving, just being present. Together. After a while, Bass wiped his face and broke the silence.

"So wait, Rebekah is my relative?"

"Yes, she's my great aunt, so your great, great aunt."

"She's crazy!" Bass exclaimed.

"You're telling me?"

We both laughed.

"And Jacob is really Mom's relative?"

"Yes, he's her great uncle I believe."

"What about Mary? Is that Mama Maria?"

"Yep," I said, "That's my mom."

"I never met her but I remember Mom talking about her a few times when I was younger." Bass paused, his eyes darting around the room, and then looked at me. "And why didn't I know it was you all along? I feel pretty dumb."

"To be fair, I look like an angel now. Actually, I am an angel. So that's part of it."

Bass nodded in agreement.

"And I have hair now. By the time you could remember anything as a kid, the chemo had already taken my hair."

"But your name, it's so obvious!"

"Is it?" I said. "You only knew me as Joe because that's what your mom and everyone called me. My birth name is Miguel Jose Martinez. You know, Miguel means Michael in Spanish," I said, smiling. "Maybe if you tried to learn more Spanish..."

"Yes Dad, I know," Bass said, rolling his eyes.

He thought for a moment. "Are the councils always made up of people's relatives? Our ancestors?"

"No, not always. But in many cases, yes. We have a vested interest in your well-being. If we have the right experience, we get called to the assignment. Mary, Rebekah, and Jacob were the right team for you. They knew how to reach you."

Bass became silent, but I knew what he was thinking.

"Not yet," I said.

"Huh?"

"Soon, but not yet. Your mom is going through what I would call 'training'. There's a lot she needs to learn. It's kind of like she just graduated from college and now she's getting started with the real work. In fact, I've been put in charge with bringing her up to speed."

"So, you've seen her?"

"Yes." Again, it was hard for me to speak. "I got to see her."

Bass processed it all—his eyes darted back and forth, tracking every thought racing through his mind.

"So it's true," he started. "There really is life after death. And God is really, you know, real? Like really real?"

I nodded and smiled.

"Am I going crazy? I mean, did I seriously just lose it? Am I hallucinating this entire thing?"

"Probably," I said.

"What?" he snapped back.

"Ha! No, I'm kidding." I put my arm around him and said, "Son, it's real. I promise. The whole thing—God, angels, this earthly journey you're on. And you're just getting started."

"Why now? Why couldn't you have been in my life sooner? There were times as a kid where I could have really used a father."

"I know," I said. I felt a familiar twinge of compassion, which bordered on guilt. "What I've been able to piece together is that this is the best time for me to be in your life. We had a lot of work to do, but now was the time when we could make the biggest difference."

"Will you get to stay with me?"

"I'm still not sure of how it all works. Our job was to help you find your life's greatest treasure. We only have a little bit of time left to help you make that happen."

"Yeah, I know. Talk about laying on the pressure. I'm still unclear on what I'm actually supposed to do."

"Well, you've got what, seven days left? That's a lot of time." I gave him a reassuring smile. "I'm sure you'll be able to find your treasure. Just focus on what you know is right."

Bass processed what I said. He looked over at Kathy's computer. I knew where his thoughts were headed.

"Dad, I miss her. I really miss her. I should have been there for her." He stopped talking, trying to keep it together.

I leaned over and put my arm around him, and he started trembling again.

"Son, I know exactly how you feel. For so many years, I was still alive but not able to be there for you or your mother. I wish I had been there for you. To see you go through school. To see you catch a wave for the first time. To see you working hard. I missed so many things. But now, I see that there's a bigger picture."

"A bigger picture?"

I took a flower, a white carnation, from the vase and looked at it. I twisted it in my fingers, looking at all the tiny petals.

"Yes, at first glance, this life looks chaotic. Like it's all random, unfair even. So much injustice in the world. So many people making poor decisions."

I turned the flower in my hand. At first, it looked like a random gathering of petals smashed together. Then I looked deeper and saw the perfect lines that governed the flowers' growth. There was order. There was beauty. Bass looked at the flower too and I could tell he also saw what I saw. It was a perfect creation.

As I held the flower close, it glowed from within. The light started from the stem and penetrated outward to every part of the petals. The light got brighter until it reached the ends of the petals and then faded.

"Whoa!" Bass said. "Did you do that?"

"Yes. I asked the flower to show us its beauty. It felt my appreciation for it so it opened up to me."

I handed the flower to Bass, and he held it delicately.

"Son, underneath it all, everything that exists, there is love. I know it. I've experienced it now myself. It just needs to be coaxed out. That's your job—to serve and to love others."

I knew it was time. I started to fade. I didn't want to. I wanted to stay longer. But the look on Bass's face told me he would be OK.

CHAPTER FORTY-FIVE

A few days after driving all of Kathy's stuff to his home, Bass got a message to meet with an attorney. He was asking to meet via an online chat. It was late afternoon when Bass hopped on the meeting.

"Hello Sebastian, thank you for taking the time to meet with me. I'm sorry I didn't get the chance to meet you while you were up here in Monterey."

"No problem," Bass said.

"I'm sorry for your loss. I knew Katherine, umm, your mother personally. She was a wonderful woman and I'm not just saying that. She helped my wife one time." The lawyer paused to find the right words. "My wife was very sick and your mother helped her to get better. I won't ever be able to thank your mother enough..." he trailed off.

The lawyer paused again to steady himself. He straightened his tie and said, "Excuse me." He sat up in his chair, cleared his throat, and focused again on Bass.

"Right. OK, just so you know, I will email all of this information over to you as well as mailing hard copies," he said.

"I'll dive into this with the most important details. Actually, let me send this doc over to you right now."

He made a few clicks, and a file popped up in the corner of Bass's laptop. He opened it to see an official-looking document that outlined the estate of Katherine Schneider Martinez.

Bass blinked hard a few times. He never knew his mother had an estate.

"Do you have the doc open?" the lawyer asked.

"Yes," Bass said, skimming it quickly.

"I'll highlight a few key points if that's OK."

"Got it."

"You'll notice that your mother is leaving literally everything she owns to you. First and foremost, she's leaving you the sum of $578,200 dollars in cash and other liquid investments, give or take a few dollars. You'll find the account details in the doc…"

Bass couldn't believe what he was hearing. His mother was leaving him with over half a million dollars. How did she even manage to save that much? He thought she was poor. Except for her fancy computer and her golf clubs, Bass figured she wasn't doing that well.

"Sebastian?"

"Yes, sorry," Bass replied.

The lawyer smiled. "Yes, I can understand. Your mother made more than she let on. It appears she was saving it all. Let me just continue," he said.

He talked about how Kathy left Bass several other smaller investments, her car, and everything she owned. He said he was to make special mention of the various family history boxes. The will stated he was supposed to ensure that Bass acknowledged them verbally.

"Yes, I've got all the boxes," Bass said. He thought for a moment and added, "And yes, they are very special to me. There's a lot of priceless information there."

"I understand," said the lawyer.

A COUNCIL OF ANGELS

Something about the way the lawyer said that made Bass feel like he really did understand. He continued to give further instructions, but Bass could hardly pay attention. His thoughts were swallowed up by his emotions. A few minutes later, he was signing off with the lawyer.

"If you need anything else, please don't hesitate to reach out to me. Your mother was a special person, truly an angel. If I can help her son in any way, it would be a pleasure for me to do so."

"Thank you very much," Bass said.

He turned from his laptop and was overwhelmed. He stood up and looked out his front room window. A small family was walking past on the sidewalk. A mother, father, and a little boy riding a bike with training wheels. They both hovered over the boy as he wobbled along.

Bass was overcome. He thought about the money. Money he could never repay to his mother. He thought about the genealogy. His mother sacrificed her time to help others, including and especially him. As he thought about her entire life since he was born, he realized just how much of it was focused on helping him.

His thoughts turned to his dad and how he saved him as a kid. He literally owed his dad his life, and he was eternally indebted to his mother for her years and years of sacrifice on his behalf. He was humbled as he realized he wasn't as self-made as he once believed he was.

Bass felt like he'd been blinded for so long by his own ambition, and that he lost sight of what his parents had actually done for him. Wanting nothing more than to see his parents again to apologize, a paralyzing sensation came over him, and his knees buckled, and he headed to the floor.

For a while, there was only darkness. Then, he saw a light. The light increased and Bass saw a beach. It was late afternoon, and the sun was sinking in the sky.

He was suddenly standing on the beach, watching the waves

come in. To his right was his dad and to his left, his mom. They looked young, like they were his same age, and they both linked their arms in his and stared at the sun. Time sped up, but Bass remained still with his mother and father next to him.

The waves came in fast, the clouds rushed past, and the sun suddenly dropped to the horizon. It slowed and shot out brilliant rays of red, orange, and yellow, turning the sky into shades of pink and purple.

As the sun was about to disappear from view, his parents moved closer and hugged him. He knew they were leaving. He didn't want them to. He tried to cry out but couldn't speak. They smiled at him and turned to look at the sun as they both faded from sight. The sun shot out a bright flash of light.

As the light changed, he saw a girl walking towards him. It seemed like the same girl from his previous dream. The sun lit her up from behind, and her entire body glowed. She got closer and smiled at him, and he felt love radiating from her.

The sun got brighter and brighter, and Bass put his hand up to block it. He closed his eyes and turned away, but it continued to fill everything with blazing light.

He opened his eyes and saw sunlight reflecting off his neighbor's window and shining in on him. As he looked around, he realized he was lying on the floor of his living room. He closed his eyes, desperately trying to go back into his dream, but it was gone.

He stood up slowly, his mind racing. A chime came from his laptop, signaling a new email. He went over to check it. The subject line read:

Your offer has been accepted.

CHAPTER FORTY-SIX

Two days after Bass spoke with his mother's attorney, he wrote out a short list with five names on it. He looked at each of the names and thought about each person in particular. He'd already made several preparations, and he smiled as he tried to imagine how each person would react. Now all he had to do was sleep.

The next morning, he woke up early. He had a big day ahead of him. He showered, got dressed, and walked out to the beach. He stood on the stairs above the sand, watched the waves come in, and basked in the morning sun. He closed his eyes and said a prayer.

"Dear God, if you can hear me, I thank you for my life. I thank you for my parents. I thank you for my council of angels. Thank you for everything they've taught me. I pray that I get my priorities in order. Please God, bless me to be able to see others and to help them. Bless me with true sight. Bless me to see people the way you see them. Today, I have a list of people who have influenced me. Please bless me to help them. Please."

Bass opened his eyes and inhaled and exhaled deeply until he got goosebumps. He turned back to his house to get his car. He had a lot to do.

The first stop was to go into the building where he used to work. He stopped by Derrick's office and knocked on the door.

"Come in," he said.

"Hey, real fast, I got you this," Bass said.

Bass gave him a bag with tissue paper in it. Derrick pulled out a coffee mug, which said, *Family Man*. He smiled and said, "Wow, I don't know what to say. Thank you, Bass."

"There's more," Bass said, pointing to the bag.

He dug in the bag and pulled out a shirt, and let out a huge laugh. The shirt read, *Mr. Tight Pants Man*.

"Look on the back."

It read, *My wife likes it. Deal with it!*

"I love it. Thank you." He stood up and gave Bass a firm handshake. "You keep in touch," he said.

"I will."

Bass moved down the hallway to Haley's office. She was putting her things into a number of boxes. Apparently the new company didn't need her after all. For a quick moment, Bass thought he could see Haley's light. It was dim. He knocked on the door and said, "I heard."

Somehow, just hearing him speak seemed to trigger Haley, and she started to cry, but Bass quickly interrupted her. "Hey, hey hold on. Did you hear my news?"

Haley shook her head no.

"Brittany's company valued my business way less than they should have. That means it didn't cost me as much to buy back Jen's share as I thought it would. I also recently received a bit of extra money that helped a lot." Bass paused for a moment, remembering his mother. "I also leased a building and a ton of equipment in San Juan Capistrano. It's farther to drive every day but it will be all mine."

"That's really great news, Bass. I'm happy for you."

"Don't you live near there? Dana Point, right?"

"Yes, we love it there."

"Yeah, well, I better go," he said. "But hey, I've got something for you."

He handed her a manila envelope. She pulled out a letter and quickly scanned it and put her hand over her mouth. She fell into her chair and looked up at Bass.

"This can't be real. Are you serious?"

"100%. I'm going to need a new director of operations," he said.

"But you don't hire people. You outsource everything."

Bass smiled. "Well, I'm hiring people now. I now see the value of having a team of good people around. And I need someone to manage all of them. I think you'll find the compensation is pretty darn good. And it's closer to home. Do you want the job?"

"Yes! When do I start?"

"How about today?"

Haley nodded yes.

"But," Bass said, "let's have you take a week off first. Get some time in with your daughter. I'll have you on the books getting paid starting now though. I mean, if that's OK with you?"

Haley stood up and practically fell on Bass. "Thank you," she said.

"Hey, I'm your boss now. Let's keep it professional."

"Oh my gosh! I'm so sorry," she said and let go.

"I'm kidding! Bring it in." Bass gave her another hug and then glanced at his watch. "I've got to run. See you next week?"

"Totally," she said. "Thank you again."

Bass took one last look at Haley. Her light was already much brighter. He turned and ran out of the office. When he got to the parking lot, he looked back at the building where he'd put in so much time. He cupped his hands together in a prayer position and made a bow to respect the opportunity he'd been blessed with for so long.

"Now, time for a new chapter," he said.

He jumped in his SUV and raced south on the freeway towards his new company home in San Juan Capistrano.

CHAPTER FORTY-SEVEN

Bass pulled into the parking lot at his new building. He saw a man already waiting there by the front door. Bass took a deep breath and whispered, "Please Lord, guide me." He looked at the angel bracelet the girl from Rome gave him as it hung on the rearview mirror.

Bass got out of the car and walked towards the man.

"Are you Dan?"

"Yes, sir."

Bass walked up and shook his hand. He looked Dan in the eyes, but Dan quickly looked away.

"You're early," Bass said. "I like that."

The two men walked into the building. Bass unlocked his office door and let Dan in.

"Sit anywhere," Bass said.

Dan pulled up a chair on the side of the room. Bass pulled up another chair and sat close to him. He noticed that Dan's suit was old, his tie was crooked, and he wore steel toe boots.

"Mr. Martinez, sir, before you start, I have to say, I'm so incredibly sorry. It was never..."

Bass held up his hand to stop him.

"Don't worry about a thing. Seriously."

"But I..." Dan started again.

Bass pulled up his pants and showed Dan some light scarring on his leg.

"See that? That's the worst of it. Really, that's it."

Dan opened his mouth and closed it again, not knowing what to say or even how to react. He sat back in his chair and scanned Bass up and down, trying to read him.

"Honestly, what happened happened. It's over," Bass said. "And to be honest, it was a wake up call for me. It was a good thing for me. A really good thing." Bass paused and lowered his voice. "Now, let's talk about you. I can't imagine it was all good for you."

Dan paused for a moment, not believing that Bass had so easily forgiven him. But thinking about the question made him look down. "No, sir," he said in a defeated tone. "It's been rough."

Bass sorted through some papers. They were from the court and showed how much Dan was going to have to pay Bass in installments. He threw them in a drawer, closed it, and looked back over to Dan.

"Tell me about your family."

"Well, we have two kids, a boy and a girl. They're both now living up in the Bay Area with their own families. Nancy and I have been married for 38 years..."

"38 years," Bass said. "That's not too common these days. What's the secret?"

Dan looked down at his feet. "Honestly, I can't tell you. I think I just got lucky with a really amazing woman." He traced a line on the floor with his boot. "It's been tough. I put us in a terrible situation. But she's stood by me." His voice cracked. "She's the one who got me through this."

"She sounds amazing."

A COUNCIL OF ANGELS

"She is."

"One more question—what are you doing these days for a job?"

"Well, I'm not allowed to drive currently, and being an electrician kind of requires that. I honestly don't know what I'm going to do."

Bass pulled out a manila envelope and gave it to Dan. He held his breath as Dan opened it and read the letter inside.

"You can't be serious."

"Yes, I am," Bass said. "I did my homework. 25 years with a company and you hardly even took a sick day. That's the kind of work ethic I love. I'm not gonna judge you by one mistake you made. I've been in touch with a cop, and I know it was a onetime thing. Besides, look at this building. I've had a couple of days to check the place out. It needs some work. I could use someone like you around here."

Dan's mouth hung open. Bass smiled back. Dan blinked quickly and then shook his head and put the letter back in the manila envelope.

"No, this can't be real. This kind of stuff doesn't happen. I think you're pulling something here."

He moved to stand up. Bass reached forward and put his hand on Dan's leg. He pushed firmly and stared right into Dan's eyes.

"This is real. I want you here. Look through the offer. It's more than what you were making at that jerk's company, anyway."

Dan allowed himself to smile at the joke, but then quickly shook his head in disbelief.

"But why? I'm the drunk driver who sent you to the hospital. Why would you do this?"

Bass took a deep breath and felt goosebumps. He looked directly at Dan and said, "You made a mistake. Simple as that. That mistake set up a chain of events that changed my life for the better. Now, I want to help you change your life for the better. What do you say?"

Dan stared out the window, and after a moment, shook his head in disbelief again. He turned back to Bass. "OK, real talk then—how does a kid like you have enough money to run an entire company like this?"

Without thinking, Bass said, "I owe everything to my parents. I am who I am because of them."

Dan nodded. Bass thought he may have misunderstood—that he was just a rich kid. He started to clarify but Dan said, "I think they taught you well."

For a moment, the two locked eyes, and Dan raised his eyebrows and smiled ever so slightly.

"So, do you want the job?"

"Yes sir, I do. Thank you. Thank you very much."

Bass stood, and Dan jumped up, shaking Bass's hand firmly with both hands.

"OK, great!" Bass said. "By the way, just call me Bass. None of that 'sir' stuff."

Dan chuckled. "OK."

They walked towards the front door and Bass added, "One more thing—a personal question."

"Anything."

"Do you still drink?"

"No way. Ironically, I never was much of a drinker. Crazy that this sort of thing happened to me."

"Well, it certainly brought about some big life changes for you and me both," Bass said. "I'm sorry for how it happened, but I'm sure grateful for the outcome."

Dan hefted the manila envelope in his hand. "I know what you mean."

"You have a ride?"

Dan looked sheepish. "Yes," he muttered. "My wife dropped me off. She's waiting for me around the corner."

"That's great. I like that. Tell her I said 'hello'. OK, so I'll see you next week."

Bass shook Dan's hand again, climbed into his SUV, and looked at his list. He still had two more visits to go. These were the fun ones.

CHAPTER FORTY-EIGHT

Bass cruised back to Huntington Beach along PCH. He had his windows down and breathed in the sweet ocean air. He thought about how much had changed. Haley and Dan would now be working for him. Others would be working for him. It was a tremendous responsibility, but he was hopeful.

He finally made it to Huntington Beach and parked in front of Pancho's Tacos. He walked up and greeted the first employee he saw.

"Hi Emma," he said.

She turned and said, "Hello!" She seemed happy that he knew her name.

"Is Pancho here?"

"Yes, let me go get him."

Minutes later, Pancho walked up to the front of the restaurant and Bass pulled out a new MP3 player and some wireless speakers.

"This," he said to Pancho, "is an MP3 player and they connect to these speakers. It's meant to replace your old CD player. That way the music will never skip."

A COUNCIL OF ANGELS

Pancho stroked his mustache skeptically, but slowly smiled. "Yes, my kids have these I think."

Bass showed him how to select different songs in the collection, which was loaded full of classical Mexican music. As Bass scrolled through the tracks, Pancho shook his head in disbelief.

"So much music! Thank you, Bass. Gracias. Muchas gracias."

"Listen to this."

Bass synched the MP3 player with the speakers and music flooded the restaurant. Pancho laughed as he heard the sound. He put his arm around Bass and yelled at the staff in the kitchen. "This man eats for free!"

"No," Bass said but Pancho insisted. Then Pancho turned to Emma and said, "Did you hear that? This man eats for free. He never pays."

Emma gave him a nod and thumbs up.

"Pancho, a little MP3 player does not equal free food," Bass said.

Pancho put his hand up to stop him.

"This song," he said, pointing to the air, "is 'Cielito Lindo' and is one of my favorite songs in the world. I take it as a sign from God that you have come to bless my restaurant." He looked at Bass and said, "Hijo mío, you eat for free. Come, sit down. I'll bring you some tacos."

"I want to, but I can't right now. But soon, I promise."

Pancho put his arm around Bass again and walked him to the front door. "I should clarify," Pancho said, "that *you* eat for free. Not your blond friend. He eats too much."

Bass laughed. "OK, I won't tell him. But if I eat for free, I'm going to leave some big tips for Emma and the muchachos in the kitchen."

Pancho lit up.

"You said muchachos. You're speaking Spanish!"

He gave Pancho a big hug and said, "Hasta luego."

"Que te vaya bien, hijo mío," Pancho replied. He stood at the door to his restaurant, with his chest puffed out, and a huge smile underneath his mustache.

Bass turned and got back in his SUV. As he pulled onto the street, he gave Pancho a wave goodbye. He still had one last stop.

CHAPTER FORTY-NINE

As Bass headed to the gym where JP worked, he sent JP a text to meet him outside in five minutes. A few minutes later, Bass pulled up to the gym and saw JP already waiting by the front doors. He was swinging his car keys, which he kept on a really long strap. Bass zipped around the parking lot, making sure his tires squealed on the pavement. JP looked over as Bass raced to a stop in front of him.

"Get in! Hurry!" Bass yelled frantically.

JP looked confused and then almost scared, and jumped in the car. Bass hit the gas and screeched out of the parking lot.

"What? What's going on?" JP yelled. "What's happening?"

Bass didn't speak, but buried his foot on the gas pedal. He got onto the main road and checked the mirrors, acting as if someone were following them. JP started doing the same. He even turned to look behind them.

"Dude, what the heck is going on?"

Bass pretended to calm down a bit. "OK, phew! Yeah, I think it's clear." He looked to the glove box and said, "JP, open that glove box."

JP reached up and opened it.

"There's a package in there. I want you to open it very carefully."

JP grabbed the package but handled it like it was a bomb. He pulled out a small wrapped box. He shredded the wrapping paper and laughed.

"A package of sporks! I love it!"

"I thought you'd like that," Bass said. "Keep looking, there's more."

Next, JP pulled out a framed picture. It was a perfectly balanced 360 degree photo of St. Peter's Square in Rome.

"What? No way! This is awesome. How did you get this shot?"

"When you were sleeping in."

"Wait a minute, why were you so serious just now? Who are you running from?" JP caught Bass with a devilish grin. "Ha, ha. Yeah, very funny."

Bass started laughing out loud. "Oh man, I got you so bad!"

"Yeah, yeah," JP said. "But seriously, thanks for the photo and the sporks. They're awesome."

"But wait, there's more."

JP looked back in the package and pulled out a manila envelope. He opened it and started laughing. He pulled out a huge handful of one-dollar bills. "Ha, that's awesome. Let me guess, there's a thousand of these, right?"

"Yep, and a bit more to add some interest. I had to go to like six different banks to make this happen."

JP threw the dollar bills into the air.

"Cash money—make it rain!"

He did that for about five seconds before Bass threatened to open the window.

"OK, OK, I'll stop. Geez."

JP put all the bills back in the envelope. It hit Bass in that moment how much his friend meant to him. JP didn't wear white clothing, but he was an angel in Bass's life.

A COUNCIL OF ANGELS

"Dude, why are you staring at me like that?"

"I want to thank you."

"No problem. I'll lend you money anytime."

"No, not for that," Bass said, "I mean, yes thank you for that. But I'm talking about in general. Just, thank you, man."

JP looked at Bass and said, "Yeah, cool. No worries, man." JP looked out the front window ahead at the road. "I think today is the best day of my life."

Bass smiled. "I know exactly how you feel."

CHAPTER FIFTY

After a quick bite to eat, Bass dropped JP back off at his gym and then headed home. He thought about Haley, Dan, Pancho, and JP, and laughed out loud. In that moment, he realized that he was truly, deeply happy. But it was more than just doing fun stuff for his friends. It was bliss. He hoped this is what heaven was like.

As he drove down PCH, he watched the palm trees flash past, silhouetted by the blue sky behind with puffy white clouds. He rolled down the window and put his arm out, moving his hand up and down in the wind. Directly ahead of him, he stared at a cloud that looked exactly like an angel with outstretched wings.

"You know we don't have wings, right?" Jacob boomed with his deep voice.

Bass almost lost control of the steering wheel and glanced around to see all of us. Mary was up front, with Jacob in the backseat behind her, me in the middle, and Rebekah sitting directly behind Bass.

"You guys always scare me!"

"Oh Bassy, don't you know by now that we come and go whenever we want?"

A COUNCIL OF ANGELS

Rebekah wore what looked like a red prom dress from the 80s, complete with puffy sleeves.

"Wow," Bass said, "you really got dressed up."

"Today is a big day," she said, looking around. "Who's going to say it? Who gets to say it? Michael?"

"Gets to say what?"

"You did it!" Rebekah blurted out. "You found your life's greatest treasure! Wahooo!"

"I did?"

"Yeah, sport. You did it. Congrats," Jacob said.

Bass pulled over to the side of the road. He turned the car off and turned in his seat to better face everyone. "I don't get it. I don't see anything. Is something supposed to happen?"

"What have we said all along?" Jacob asked.

Bass stared down at his hands, thinking. They taught him a lot. He couldn't pin down any one thing. Rebekah gave a loud sigh.

"What have I taught you this whole time, Bassy?"

"To love?"

"Yes. How?"

Everyone focused on Bass. He looked to Mary and then at me. I nodded my head, encouraging him.

"Love by serving?"

"Exactly," Rebekah said. "And you just spent a day serving. You spent an entire day loving people. And you want to know what that kind of lifestyle leads to, Bassy?"

Bass nodded his head yes. "It means living happily ever after."

"Yes!" Rebekah exclaimed. "It means getting to live your joyous, wonderful, blissful happily ever after."

"Doesn't a happily ever after usually involve...you know... getting the girl?"

"Of course it does," Rebekah said. "But we needed you to step up and find your treasure first."

237

"Now I'm even more confused. Can somebody just tell me what my treasure is?"

I wanted to, but looked at Mary.

"What do you think it could be?" Mary asked.

He glanced around at everyone, hoping for some clue. Jacob nodded his head, rooting for Bass.

"I guess...well...I'm not sure. I used to think it was selling my company, but now I think it's more about helping others."

"What else?" Mary asked. "How have you changed?"

"Well, I've tried to look outwards and help others."

Mary pushed further. "Has that changed you in any way?"

"I think so. I hope so. I mean, JP seems to think so. He told me one time." Bass glimpsed himself in the rearview mirror and had to do a double-take when he saw his eyes. They seemed to glow. "You guys tell me if I'm wrong, but I kind of feel like maybe I'm becoming the person that God wants me to become."

"Yes!" Rebekah shouted. "I told you so! I knew he could do it."

"You're correct, Sebastian," Mary said. "Your treasure was becoming the person God wanted you to become. Or, said in another way, to be the person God knows you can be. That, Sebastian, is your life's greatest treasure, and it's going to bless you for the rest of your life."

"You're functioning at 100% Bass," Jacob said. "I knew you could do it, champ."

"And I might add that you've become the man your parents always hoped you would be," I said.

Bass looked at me, smiling. He was happy. I was too.

"Here's a question then," Bass said. "Why all the effort? I mean, wouldn't all of this just kind of happen on its own?"

"Not always," Mary said. "And not on the path you were on."

"Besides, we've got someone special in store for you, boy," Jacob said.

Bass perked up. "You do?"

"Yeah, but she's amazing, Bassy," Rebekah said. "We needed

A COUNCIL OF ANGELS

you to change, to become better. You needed to be worthy of meeting her."

"Worthy?" Bass repeated.

"Yes, worthy!" Rebekah said louder, driving in the point. "It's like when you helped the blind man—that qualified you to meet with us. Now, everything you've done has prepared you to meet her."

Jacob nodded. "If you could see all that we see, you'd realize that girls like this are pretty rare. But don't worry, you passed the test."

"When will I meet her?"

"When you least expect it," Jacob said.

"Seriously? Haven't I done enough? Can't you give me something? You are all-knowing, after all."

Everyone looked at me. "Bass, son, it'll be better if we don't tell you. Why ruin the fun? But," I added, "I can tell you it will be soon."

Bass sat back in his seat, taking in everything we told him. He opened his mouth to say something, but stopped.

"What is it?" I prodded.

"So, is this what all angels help people do—help them become the people God knows they can be?"

Everyone looked to Mary.

"Something like that," she said. "Every assignment that any angel is given is dedicated entirely to helping that person become happier in some vital way. It's our entire job."

"And," Rebekah chimed in, "this was a special assignment for us because we're your family. And, I believe there's one of us who benefitted from this experience as much as you did." She smiled as she put an arm around my shoulders.

As Rebekah said that, it hit me that she was right. This entire experience was as much for me as it was for Bass. I nodded. "Apparently, I still had some stuff to learn, too."

Bass studied my face as he thought about what I meant. I could tell from the look in his eyes he understood.

"So, what do I do now?"

"Keep doing what you're doing," Mary said.

"Yeah, keep loving!" Rebekah said. She tossed Bass's hair and disappeared. Jacob gave Bass a wink and also disappeared. Mary put a hand on Bass's leg and said, "Well done," and then faded away.

"Wait," Bass said, turning to look at me. "Hold on! Don't go. I mean, will I see you guys again?"

"Count on it," I said. I felt myself disappearing but quickly added, "I can hardly wait to see what happens next."

CHAPTER FIFTY-ONE

The next day, Bass sat on the steps at the park just north of the pier. He was thinking about everything that happened after meeting the angels. It had only been 40 days since officially saying yes to their invitation, and so much had changed in that time.

He saw a pack of boys on their bikes racing quickly towards him and noticed one boy lagging a little behind the rest. The boy stood up to pedal faster. Just as he did, his front tire hit a patch of sand and turned sideways, sending him flying over the handlebars.

Bass jumped up and rushed over to help. The boy had his hands covering his knee.

"Dude, are you OK?"

The boy looked up at Bass, holding back tears, trying to be tough. "Yeah," he whispered.

"Here, let me help you up. It's best to walk it off."

Bass helped the boy to his feet and walked with him for a few steps. Then he lifted the bike but noticed the handlebars were crooked. He put the tire between his legs and twisted the handlebars straight again.

"There," Bass said. "I think you should be good now."

"Thanks," the kid replied and got on his bicycle to catch up to his friends.

Bass watched him ride off and thought, *It does feel good to help people.* Then he turned around and almost walked right into a girl.

"Whoa, sorry," he said.

The girl stood facing him, calmly. Intentionally. He looked into her eyes. They were bright green. She smiled. Then it hit him. It was the girl from the airport. Impossible. He couldn't believe it!

"I know you," Bass began. His voice came out higher than he wanted it to. He cleared his throat and said, this time in a deeper voice, "I saw you in Europe."

The girl nodded.

"You blew me a kiss in the airport."

The girl nodded again.

"What's your name?"

"Skylar."

What a cool name, Bass thought. *And her voice, amazing.*

"Do you have a name?" she asked back.

"It's Sebastian, but everyone calls me Bass."

"Like the fish?"

"Exactly."

She looked down and said, "You're missing half a toenail. What's up with that?"

"It's a long story."

"I'd like to hear it."

CHAPTER FIFTY-TWO

The day after meeting Skylar, Bass woke up with an urge to go surfing. He needed some time in the ocean to process everything. He quickly changed, ran downstairs, and moved through the living room towards the garage, but something caught his eye.

His mom's computer was on. He previously set it up after bringing it down from Monterey. The three-screen setup was glowing, but he didn't see any programs running. Bass looked around. "Hello? Is anyone here right now?" No answer came.

Bass spotted the boxes of family history by the computer. He hadn't yet organized them, but noticed one of the boxes was open. He looked inside and saw it was full of pictures of him as a kid that he'd never seen before.

"Nope, I can't do this right now." He smiled and said, "I'm tired of crying." He put the lid back on the box and started for the garage, but stopped and looked around again. "Mom, if you can hear me, you win. I'll get busy with this soon. I promise."

Before running to the beach, there was something Bass needed to do first. He headed to his favorite surf shop and bought a new surfboard, a nine foot white longboard with a light blue trim.

The guys from the shop put the fins on, attached the leash, and waxed it up. Bass walked out to his SUV and put the board inside the back window. The sweet scent of the surfboard wax filled his car, and he breathed it in deeply.

He parked by 17th street, grabbed the board, and jogged down the beach. He paddled out through the sets of waves and rested on his board, relaxing. Skylar's face kept flashing through his mind, and he laughed out loud, thinking about her and the afternoon they shared together.

Skylar told him about seeing him in London and then in Barcelona and again at the London airport. He hadn't known about the time in Barcelona.

Bass laid back on his longboard and closed his eyes. He let the waves gently rock him and loved the sound of the water lapping up against his board.

"I thought you said longboards are for old men?" a voice boomed.

Bass smiled, opened his eyes, and saw Jacob sitting on his white longboard.

"And for bald German angels, too, I guess," Bass replied.

Then Rebekah, Mary, and I appeared too. Everyone was on their own surfboard, including me. Although I'd never done it before, somehow I balanced perfectly while sitting on the surfboard in the water. It felt natural, and I instantly saw why Bass liked it so much. Like Jacob, I wore white board shorts which practically glowed in the greenish blue water.

Mary was wearing her white robes as usual, but they remained dry, unaffected by the water. Rebekah was the only one on a shortboard, which was all red. She wore a wetsuit which was also red but had large black spots on it.

"Yes, Bassy, go ahead and stare. It's a ladybug wetsuit, and it's *amaaaazing!*"

Bass sat up on his board as we paddled our surfboards into a circle with everyone facing each other.

A COUNCIL OF ANGELS

"I've got to ask," Bass said, "did you know all of this stuff would happen all along? I mean, did I even really have a say in it all?"

"Yes," Mary said, "we certainly prompted you, but you were the one to make your own decisions and take action. We can't and never would do that for you."

Bass peered into the water and saw some fish gathering underneath his board. They darted in and out between the feet of the council.

Bass raised his hand. "I've got to confess something...I'm sorry."

Rebekah leaned forward on her board, cupping her chin with her hands. "Sorry for what?"

"I'm sorry I wasn't as nice as I should have been to you guys at the beginning. I had no idea who you were. Honestly, I thought I was losing my mind. I'm really, incredibly, super, grateful for what you've done."

"It was our pleasure, Sebastian," Mary said.

"Now that I've found this, I'm afraid I'll fall. I'm afraid I won't be able to keep this up."

"Of course you're going to fall," Jacob said. "That's part of life, tiger. The true test is how many times you'll get back up."

"And how many others you can love along the way," Rebekah added.

"It's still hard for me to believe all of this," he said, looking at me. "I mean, I know it's real but part of me still almost feels like I'm imagining it all."

"What about meeting Skylar?" Rebekah asked. "Was that real?"

Bass thought about it. Honestly, he felt like that was a dream, too. But it was real—it had actually happened.

"Yeah, that was super cool," he said.

"What about Dan? What about Haley? What about your company?" Rebekah asked.

245

Bass saw where she was going. "Yes, my life is drastically different now. In fact, it's amazing."

"Think about what you've learned," Mary said. "You know that God is real. You know that families go on after death. You know that you have the ability to make a direct, positive impact in someone's life. You cannot stay the same person after the experiences you've had."

"Here's all the proof I need," Jacob said as he tapped on Bass's longboard.

Bass laughed. "Yeah, I never thought I'd see the day when I'd be riding a longboard." He rubbed the new board with his hand. "I think I like it though."

He locked eyes with Mary. "So now that I've changed, do you think Skylar is worthy of me?"

Rebekah did a face-palm, and Jacob groaned. Mary leaned forward and said calmly but deliberately, "That's not the question you should be asking, Sebastian."

"What is, then?"

"The question you need to be asking yourself is whether or not you're worthy of her." Mary let her words sink in for a minute while Rebekah nodded emphatically.

"In fact, you should always keep that in mind for the rest of your life. Perhaps we need to teach you a lesson in humility," Mary said. "Jacob, would you like to get a big wave ready?"

Bass held his hands up. "No, no, I get it." He hit himself on the forehead and quickly glanced over at me, hoping somehow I hadn't heard. "But does this mean that she and I are going to, you know, fall in love and get married and all that?"

"That story is just beginning," I said. "But you've been prepared to meet her. Think about it—you didn't meet her until *after* you became who you needed to be. You already know how many times your paths crossed, but you weren't ready yet."

Bass thought about it. He could have met her in London,

twice. Or he could have met her in Barcelona. Or he could have met her in Huntington Beach all along. So close, but he never met her.

"Here's something else to think about," Rebekah jumped in. "Every single time the lovely Skylar saw you, you were doing something good. You were serving. Are you beginning to understand what I've been saying all along?"

Bass nodded, but Rebekah pushed further.

"You needed to be worthy of this. To do that, you needed to love, to actually practice *loving* people. And that's part of what we told you along the way. Love serves, Bassy."

Bass nodded and realized she was right, but something occurred to him.

"Wouldn't anyone do what I did, though? Like, wouldn't anyone help a lady in a wheelchair?"

"You'd be surprised," Jacob said.

"But everything that happened seemed so coincidental. I mean, I'm grateful, but isn't it crazy that Skylar just happened to be there as I was helping someone?"

I looked to Mary, and she nodded back.

"Son," I said, "you'll learn more about Skylar soon enough, but there are no coincidences. And every time you did something, you chose to do that. It was all you."

Rebekah jumped in. "Do you see how a series of making the correct decisions and choosing to serve others launched you out into this really fantastic place? You became the person you needed to be." She cupped her hand and whispered, "I always knew you would."

Bass stared down at his board, thinking. "So, in a way, it's like Skylar is a reward or something?"

"No," Mary said. "You became the person God knew you could be and as a result, you lifted yourself to another plane—the same plane where Skylar already was."

"So, she's some sort of superwoman?"

"Oh no. She's got her own work to do," Rebekah said. She glanced at me and then back to Bass. She spoke almost solemnly. "In fact, I sense that she has a long road ahead of her." Rebekah's voice trailed off. It was the first time Bass saw her speak so seriously. She looked up at him and said, "But, she'll have a fantastic partner, won't she?"

Bass nodded his head.

"Tell you what, here's my final lesson," Jacob said. "Your happily ever after will only stay with you as you continue to serve and love those around you. Stop doing that? Your life will plummet. Keep doing that? Your life will be full of happiness."

"Thank you," Bass said. "That makes a lot of sense."

Rebekah paddled closer to Bass and said, "You want to know my final lesson?" She didn't wait for Bass to reply. "If you want to have any kind of chance with Skylar, you need to treat her like a queen. *A queen*, Bassy. Remember, to serve is to love and to love is to serve."

Rebekah looked over to Mary, who studied Bass's face. After a moment she said, "I already know what you're thinking, Sebastian. Don't worry. You won't ever be alone again."

Bass's chin dropped, and he looked down at his surfboard again. Mary struck a nerve.

"Remember," she said, "you have your own council of earthly angels. Think about JP. He's the best kind of friend anyone could ask for. And you'll find that Skylar will be an angel in your life."

Bass focused on me, expecting some parting words.

I smiled. "I get to see you again tomorrow. We'll chat then."

Bass glanced around and shook his head from side to side. "I don't want you to go," he said. He struggled to speak. "An aunt, an uncle, a grandmother…and a father. It's not fair. I wish you could stay with me and help me."

"We'll always be with you, sport," Jacob said. "Just remember

A COUNCIL OF ANGELS

these experiences. Work hard. Live an honorable life. We'll be together again soon enough."

Jacob quickly made eye contact with the other angels, who all nodded in agreement. Then he put his hands in the water, and as he whispered some words, Bass realized he was saying a prayer. Bass also closed his eyes, but before he knew it, his board was moving toward a large set of waves coming in. Bass and the angels paddled to get into position.

Bass looked out and saw a monster wave taking shape. Rebekah was out in front and shouted, "Wahooo!" as she was the first to catch it. In turn, everyone also got up and rode the wave. Bass got up on his board and I followed behind.

We all rode the wave in perfect unison. Jacob rode the nose of his board while Mary crouched down and put a hand into the face of the wave next to her. Rebekah did a handstand and shouted out. Then she pushed off the board into the air and disappeared, signing 'I love you' to Bass.

Jacob cut back into the wave and simply pointed at Bass as he disappeared. Mary stood up straight on her board, put a hand over her heart, and bowed slightly towards Bass and disappeared.

The wave closed out, and Bass looked back to see if I was still there. I was. Just then, he tilted wrong and his board buried itself in the water. He went flying headfirst just as the wave broke over him. I immediately jumped off my board and dove in after him.

The monster wave thrashed around, but I managed to grab his ankle and pulled him up to the surface. We were already close to the beach, and he was able to stand. He dragged his board towards him and collapsed on it, breathing deeply.

He chuckled sheepishly. "I guess I'm not totally used to that longboard!"

"I wish I could give you some pointers, but I was never a surfer."

"Should we paddle back out and catch some more?"

249

I wanted to, I really wanted to, but I knew it was time. "Son, I've got to go."

"What? No. I get to see you again though, right?"

"Yes, there's still something amazing I get to be present for."

"Soon?"

"Yes, my boy," I said. "I promise."

CHAPTER FIFTY-THREE

The day after Bass said goodbye to the council, I got to see him for the last time. I found him on the beach near 17th street. He sat on his surfboard, gazing out to the waves.

I appeared next to him. "Lazy surf bum. Don't you ever work?"

He looked up, excited to see me. "Dad!"

"Can I sit here?"

"Yes, please!"

I sat next to him and stared out at the waves. I expected him to have a lot of questions, but he was quiet. I was content to sit there with him and enjoy the moment.

After watching the waves for a few minutes, Bass turned to me. "Can I ask you something?"

"Shoot."

"Why don't more people talk about this stuff? I mean, having a council of angels is super cool. You guys changed my life. After this is over, are you going to swear me to secrecy or something?"

"Nope, none of this is secret. There are plenty of people talking about guardian angels. People have written entire books about the experiences they've had. The real question is, how many people are actually listening?"

Bass pondered the question.

"Besides," I added, "actions are always louder than words, my boy. When you open the door for someone, or say a friendly word or two, or help push-start a car, you're helping to spread a little bit of heaven right here on earth. Your positive daily actions can have a powerful effect. Does that make sense?"

Bass nodded his head. "Yeah, it makes sense. I get it."

"But if you really want to write a book or talk to a reporter, go for it!"

"No, you're right. I mean, what would the reporter say? 'Local surfer says his dead dad teaches him the secret to life?' It sounds pretty nuts." He dug his toes into the sand and looked back at me. "Can I ask you another question? I mean, I'm pretty sure I already know the answer, but I gotta ask."

"Shoot."

"The cop in charge of my accident investigation sent me a very interesting photo a little while ago. Were you there when Dan hit me? I mean, did you make it so that he didn't hit me directly?"

I wasn't sure if he remembered that or not. I wanted to answer but couldn't find my voice. I simply nodded yes.

"That's what I thought," he said.

I could tell he was trying to get something else out. He dug his toes deeper into the sand and took a deep breath. "You saved my life as a kid and, as a result, you lost your own li—" He took another deep breath and continued. "Then you saved my life yet again. How can I ever repay you?"

I shrugged. "You can't. But it doesn't matter. Ask any good parent out there—they would do the same thing. I promise you. As JP would say, it's probably written in some handbook."

A seagull landed next to us and walked directly towards me. I

A COUNCIL OF ANGELS

wondered if it could see me. I still had a lot to learn about being an angel.

"But," I said, "if you're feeling indebted, you can remember this as you live your happily ever after. You'll need to think about your family. You'll need to think about your legacy. What do you want that to be like? It's something to ponder but most importantly, *do*. Nothing will ever be more important than family and your actions must always reflect that, son."

Bass nodded. We watched as the seagull circled around me and next to Bass. It folded its legs and sat down, seeming to enjoy Bass's company. It made Bass smile.

"Can I ask you another question?"

"Shoot."

"What was your job in all of this? If I remember right, the others called you a secretary angel or something. What does that mean?"

In an instant, I thought about the entire journey—from the car wreck, to Europe, to Kathy, to meeting Skylar, including all the changes Bass made.

"Basically, I had the immense privilege of being there for the entire thing."

"Everything? Like, since I first met you guys?"

"Even before, actually."

"Geez! I'm glad I didn't do anything really dumb."

"Oh, you did."

We both chuckled.

Bass grew silent as his gaze returned to the waves. After a minute, he turned and said, "Dad, this has been really special for me. I mean, special doesn't even begin to describe it. It's been...sacred. Thank you."

I reached over and put my arm around his shoulders.

"No," I said, "thank you. I'm so happy to have been part of your journey."

The three of us continued to look out at the ocean—Bass, myself, and the seagull.

"Hey, would you like to see something cool?"

"Of course!" Bass replied.

I pointed out to the waves, just past where they were breaking. The clouds parted enough for a bright beam of sun to shoot down to the water. It caught the spray of the waves and shot into a million different colors. Bursting through the colors, a dolphin jumped high into the air. It did a full flip before splashing back into the water.

"Wow!" Bass shouted. "Did you do that?"

"Nope. I just knew it would happen. Now, check out your surfboard."

Bass looked down and saw an angel emblem in the middle of the board towards the top.

"Whoa! How'd you do that? Wait, it doesn't matter. But I thought you guys didn't do the whole angels-with-wings thing?"

"Well, I figured it would be nice to have it match the bracelet you got from that sweet girl in Rome."

"Thank you, Dad. It's awesome."

I knew it was time. Somehow, Bass sensed it too. He sat forward on his board and said, "No. Please. Dad, don't go. Can't we have more time?"

I ached inside, but somehow knew I'd see him again. I stood and lifted him up. I pulled him close and gave him the best hug I can remember ever giving him. It was like God was hugging Bass directly through me.

"I love you, my boy. You've become the man I knew you could be. Now, it's time for the next chapter."

Bass pulled away, opened his mouth to speak, but couldn't find the right words. All he said was, "Thank you. Thank you so much."

I stood in front of my son one last time when I felt the light calling me. As I began to fade, Skylar walked into view. Bass was stunned when he saw her. She smiled, but there was something more. She was glowing. Bass instantly remembered Rome and the people he saw there. As he focused on Skylar, her light glowed brighter than anyone he'd seen before.

Before I left entirely, I put a hand on Bass's shoulder and whispered into his ear. "Son, in case you didn't know it, that, right there, is what heaven looks like."

Skylar stopped and stared at Bass.

"What's up?"

"Oh, nothing," he replied.

"You sure?"

"Yeah," he said. "I think I just realized I'm the luckiest guy in the entire world."

Skylar smiled again and Bass realized she was wearing a wetsuit and had a longboard tucked under her arm. It was cream colored with a logo of a red dolphin in the middle.

"Wait a minute, how'd you know I'd be surfing right now?"

Skylar shrugged her shoulders and said, "Just a hunch."

"And…you surf, too?"

"Yes. Yes I do, Mr. Martinez." Skylar eyed Bass's brand new longboard. "I see you're a longboard kind of guy. Nice."

"I just bought it," Bass said.

"I can tell."

Bass stood, almost dumbfounded. He stared at Skylar, hoping that it wasn't a dream. He bit down hard on the inside of his cheek. It wasn't.

The smile on Skylar's face faded just a bit, and she tilted her head and asked, "What is it?"

"I'm not the luckiest guy in the entire world," Bass said. His throat tightened, and he could barely get the words out. "I'm the luckiest guy in the entire universe."

Skylar leaned in and kissed him on his cheek. A jolt of electricity raced down his spine.

He swung around to look at the sets coming in. The waves

were shoulder high and breaking right, his favorite. He closed his eyes, took a deep breath in through his nose, and let it out slowly through his mouth. He knew that his happily ever after had just begun. He opened his eyes to see Skylar smiling at him.

"Shall we?" she asked.

"Definitely."

CHAPTER FIFTY-FOUR

Well, my sweetest friend, have you ever seen an angel? Of course you have!

Now you know more about the work our son Bass did and the work he's about to embark on. He found his treasure.

And now, my beautiful Katherine, I hope this report gives you some insight into our son's life. As you know, he's special. And what a wonderful girl he now has!

I cannot put into words how grateful I am to have worked with Bass so closely. It's changed who I am. I love him. I'm so proud to be his father.

It's time to wrap up this report. I believe you've got your first assignment coming up, and I just found out that we get to work on it together. Imagine that!

I can tell you, Katherine, I thought nothing could move me more than working with our son, but this new assignment has really opened my eyes to the bigger picture.

For the first time since my death, I have hope. Now I fully understand this precious truth—that our dear family goes on. Death did not separate us. Our family is eternal. We are part of them and they are part of us. It always has been and will always be so.

In this service as an angel, I've learned more about God's love than in any other experience I've ever had. Every single one of us is so loved and there's a plan for each one of us—even if it takes a council of angels to make it happen.

Read on for the first two chapters of

A FAMILY OF ANGELS

By Sean Marshall

∼

Book Two in the Council of Angels Series

Turn the page to continue reading Skylar's story…

CHAPTER ONE

Do you know where babies go when they die? I didn't until recently, but it puts my soul at ease to know that it's the same for all young children. The reason I'm writing this report directly to you, Michael, is to give you some necessary background on Skylar McBride. I'm sure you're aware by now that she's your future daughter-in-law, and I hope this information helps you to understand how special she is.

I can't tell you how much I loved reading your report on Bass. It was so illuminating to see how everything in his life lined up so that he could meet Skylar, with your help of course. Now, I hope to give you my own detailed, firsthand account of what happened with her side of the story. I pray that by sharing my report with you, as well as adding it to the archives, together we can share the wisdom to better assist the entire human family, and do our part as angels to lift those whom we love and serve.

If I had to describe Skylar in one word, it would be lovely. Really, you're going to adore her.

Having served on a council of angels, you know all of this already, but unlike you, I've never been a secretary angel—as any kind of angel, for that matter. This was the first council I've been assigned to, and I was astonished by what it allowed me to see and feel. I experienced the world through Skylar's physical senses, lived the thoughts as they raced through her mind, and felt every emotion that pumped through her heart.

I now understand why having the assignment of secretary angel is so highly sought after—you get the rare opportunity to experience a human connection, an intimate knowledge, that I will never be able to fully explain in words. What a blessing to be so close to someone we love so much!

If you don't mind, I'm going to model what you did in your previous report on Bass, by jotting down all of the key moments that I witnessed firsthand in Skylar's life. And just like you did with Bass's report, I'm going to share as much of this through her point of view as possible. I bounce in and out of the scenes a little, but like you were with Bass, I was always present, getting to watch and record everything with Skylar.

This is her story. I hope you enjoy it.

CHAPTER TWO

To get things started, I'm going to borrow some details from the report of another angel who witnessed the events involving Skylar first hand. I visited Memorial park in Cupertino, California where this key event took place. I wanted to observe everything for myself so I could better understand Skylar's experience.

I stood near the parking lot within view of the main street, Stevens Creek Blvd. As I read the report, the events of the day supernaturally unfolded before me. I could clearly see everyone as if I had been there at the same time, and more importantly, I could hear every thought and feel every emotion of the people I chose to focus on.

I was immediately drawn to a young family unloading their truck for the day's activities, so I moved in closer to get a better look. I first noticed the father, Owen, wearing flip flops, cargo shorts, with sunglasses resting on his light brown hair. He heaved a large cooler onto the grass. The mother, Claudia, was near the back of the truck holding tightly onto a leash attached around the neck of a young husky pup. Their son, 10 years old, wore his favorite yellow shirt, and had a lollipop in his mouth. He saw the puppy and jumped out of the backseat of the truck and raced around to where his mother stood.

"I wanna hold Denali!" he exclaimed. "He's my dog. Can I? Can I please hold him?"

The husky barked and tried to jump up on the boy, but Claudia pulled back hard on the leash which made the puppy yelp.

"Mom," the boy cried, "you're hurting him!"

"No, sweetie," she replied calmly, "I'm training him."

She walked to the table where the boy's 12-year-old sister, Ava, sat with her head buried in her phone, texting feverishly.

Claudia sat down, waved to her son, and said, "Come here. Put the leash around your wrist and do not let go. Understand?"

"Yeah, yeah, I got it," the boy said quickly, already anticipating running on the grass with his new best friend.

"He's still small, but he's strong so you have to hold on tight."

"Yeah, I know," he said, already trying to walk away.

Claudia grabbed his hand and said, "I'm serious. Denali is a puppy, *and* he's a husky. That means he's got even more energy than you do."

"I know, Mom. I got it."

"OK," she said and let go of her son. She watched as they took off running together.

Owen caught her smiling and said, "A boy and his dog. Classic."

"I don't know about this," she replied. "He's only 10. I'm not sure if he can handle the responsibility."

"He'll be fine. Nobody loves animals more than that kid. The dog is long overdue," he said turning to a pile of heavy-duty multicolored nylon. "But I still say he's too old for a bounce house, though."

"It's the least we can do for celebrating his birthday over two weeks late," she replied.

A COUNCIL OF ANGELS

"I suppose," Owen said. "Wanna help me get this thing set up?"

As I fast-forwarded through the report, I watched more people arrive, all carrying presents that formed a giant mound on the table. As the kids spilled into the park, they all made a beeline to the bounce house. I watched as everyone ate, laughed, and finally sang to the birthday boy after which he blew out the candles on his cake.

Time slowed back to normal as a flock of Canada geese waddled closer and closer to the festivities. Denali was tethered by his leash, which was attached to a post in the ground. He barked loudly at the geese and paced back and forth, pulling hard at the leash, and whining loudly between barks.

"Mom," the boy said leaving his cake and walking over to Denali, "he wants off his leash. It's hurting him."

"Son, I promise it's not hurting him. Huskies just whine loudly. He's fine."

The geese waddled closer, prompting Denali to bark even louder.

"Mom, please. Let me take him. I'll hold his leash, OK?"

Claudia was about to reply when two other moms wrapped their arms around her and took a selfie.

"I wasn't ready," she said laughing. "Take another one."

I looked back to the boy who had already removed the leash from the post. The moment Denali knew he was free, he shot out towards the geese. The boy lost his grip on the leash and fell to the ground. He got up quickly and chased after the husky who bolted away. The geese immediately took flight but were still tantalizingly close to the ground. Denali jumped and nipped at a bird in the back of the flock. He missed but continued to run at full speed.

The boy yelled, "Denali, come back!"

He ran as fast as he could to catch up. The geese turned to avoid a tree as they climbed higher into the air with Denali just behind. They flew over Stevens Creek Blvd and Denali launched into the street, oblivious to the cars flashing past.

The party goers were startled by an SUV's long and loud honk, and everyone looked in its direction. They saw a silver Toyota Camry as it swerved at the last minute to avoid the puppy. The dog escaped collision, but at the exact same time, Claudia watched her baby boy roll up the hood of the silver car and slam into the windshield. The force of the impact sent him flying into the air, his body flailing up and over the car until he hit the asphalt with a sickening thud where he lay motionless.

Claudia tried to move, but her feet disobeyed. She wanted to run, but couldn't. She saw the silver car screech to a halt and hit the sidewalk.

"My son!" a man shouted.

Claudia turned to see Owen sprinting at full speed towards the street. She tried to move but still, her legs refused. Stuck, she watched Owen fall to the road in front of her son. She saw him on his knees, bent over their child, blocking her view of what was happening.

Then she heard it. It was soft at first but grew with each millisecond. A moan. A groan. A long guttural cry. It came from Owen and she refused to listen. Then the words came snaking along the wind, into her ears and down to her heart.

"No. Noooooo!" Owen cried.

Claudia knew. Somehow she already knew. Her precious boy was gone. Suddenly, her legs released from their concrete grip but instead of running, she dropped to the ground. Her vision started to cloud when she sensed someone with her. It was Ava.

"Mom," she said, her voice trembling, "what's happening?"

Claudia pulled Ava in close and gasped for air. Her eyes blurred. She felt Ava shaking in her arms. Something in Claudia snapped and she knew she had to be strong. She had to be strong for Ava, for her family. She stroked Ava's hair and began to shush her.

A COUNCIL OF ANGELS

"It's OK, sweetie. It's gonna be OK."

Claudia watched as more people ran to the street. She could see Owen's body shaking as he held their boy in his arms. She knew she needed to be there for him. Claudia began to stand as one of her friends grabbed Ava and wrapped the trembling girl in her arms. Claudia walked forcefully to the street, each step a colossal feat.

As she got closer, the door of the silver car caught her attention. It opened slowly and Claudia saw a girl grip the top of the door to stand. She was young, probably around 16 years old, her face was pale and lifeless. Claudia instinctively turned towards her.

Looking fearfully at the crowd gathering around the boy, the girl whispered something but then her eyes rolled back in her head and she passed out, hitting the sidewalk beneath her.

DID YOU LIKE THE BOOK?

If you found *A Council of Angels* enjoyable, inspirational, uplifting, or otherwise fun and happy in any way, would you please consider leaving a review online? Amazon is the best place, really.

It will help take this message to others who may need to hear something found in the pages of this book.

If you do leave an honest review, please know that I'm giving you a virtual hug. Thank you!

SPECIAL THANKS

I would like to thank my advance team of readers and critics including Chelsea Valentine, Julie and Todd Taggart (& family), Wendi Johnson, Pawel Konczyk, Emily Egge, and Benjamin Marshall. Thank you for your honest opinions and encouragement.

I would like to also thank my parents, David and Mary Sue Marshall, for instilling in me a love of good books at a young age.

Additionally, I would like to thank Holli Gutierrez for your time and expertise applied to this book. Also, a big thank you to Jennifer Wright—editing is definitely one of your talents. And also, thank you to Pamela Capone for all of your suggestions and time spent on this project. I owe you a bucket of gnocchi!

And to my own sweetest friend, Heidi, for being patient, supportive, and applying your faith to making this happen. I could not have done this without you. Seriously.

Finally, to my Creator for giving me a truly abundant life, a happy & healthy family, and the ability to share this story with others.

ABOUT THE AUTHOR

Together with his beautiful wife and three fantastic children, Sean Marshall enjoys people watching at airports, quoting funny movies, and putting too much brown sugar on his morning oatmeal.

He calls Southern California home but claims he's left pieces of his soul in Scotland, Spain, and Mexico—all places where he & his family have lived for the better part of the last decade.

~

For a chance to win free stuff or to say hola, connect with him at seanmarshall.com

~

If you would like to be part of Sean's Advance Reader Team, email him at: Sean@SeanMarshall.com

SHARE YOUR STORY

It's my wish that everyone could work with their very own council of angels at some point in their life. I do personally believe in angels, and I also believe that they are nearest when our need is greatest.

I've already received many very special emails from people who have shared how the messages found within these books helped them in some way—from people reconnecting with estranged parents to striving to make good deeds a daily practice to controlling their own negative emotions and actions for fear of upsetting their council of angels!

I can't tell you how much I love getting these emails!

If you have any experiences with angels, or just happy thoughts and you'd like to share them, please send me an email at: Sean@SeanMarshall.com

Made in the USA
Middletown, DE
27 November 2022